# JEAL... WITCH

## MIDLIFE IN MOSSWOOD BOOK 2

louisa west romance

# JEALOUSY'S A
# WITCH

MIDLIFE IN MOSSWOOD BOOK 2

# LOUISA WEST

Edited by Kimberly Jaye

Proofread by Lindsay Aggiss

Cover design by Louisa West

*For those who just need a little hope.*

Find out who you are, and do it on purpose.

— DOLLY PARTON

# CHAPTER ONE

I t felt as though the whole world was holding its breath. Aside from the sound of Maggie singing to herself inside the cottage and the hiss and spit of the meat on the grill, everything was silent. Even the boys painting the house had stopped their chatter, turning to peer at the new arrival with unrestrained interest. Rosie looked from Tammy to Declan and then back again, trying to simultaneously assess the situation and form a plan before everything went to hell in a handbasket.

But life was never meant to be that easy—or at least hers wasn't. Rosie tried to take a deep breath, but the air around her was robbed of oxygen. Instead the atmosphere was charged with all the tension of a gathering storm, as though everything in her life had been leading her right up to that very moment. All of the disappointments and heartbreaks she had suffered seemed like training hurdles, and as her eyes met Tammy's she knew that this situation was somehow the test she hadn't realized she'd been waiting for all along. Her own energy seemed to twist and turn inside of her, rushing to the edge of release before shying back away from the final leap.

She thought back to the day she had met Tammy, huddled amongst the stronger personalities of Priscilla Bishop, the Pastor's wife, and Leanne Coombes as they had invaded her home under the guise of welcoming her to Mosswood. She had seemed like the only genuine person in the bunch. Rosie had felt terrible when Tammy had seen her husband Terry making a pass at her the day he'd come out to the cottage to 'offer his services' as a handyman. She hadn't seen her since that day, but it didn't look like things had improved for her any.

Tammy looked sheepishly between Declan and Rosie, her knuckles tight around the laundry bag of clothes she held in front of her like a trick or treat sack.

"I don't mean to impose," she said softly, even though it was clear that she knew she was. "I hoped that...well!" Unshed tears suddenly welled in her eyes, and she tried a combination of blinking and fanning her wedding-ring devoid hand in front of her face to stop them from falling.

Declan shifted uncomfortably beside the grill. He

turned his attention to the meat intently, but Rosie could see the tense setting of his shoulders. Tammy was glancing between the pair of them, clearly embarrassed and unsure of what to say or do.

Rosie's heart squeezed for Tammy. She wasn't one to leave someone in distress without a shoulder to cry on, and as she took her first step across the lawn it felt as though something deep inside of her resonated with her decision to help Tammy. She crossed to the table and set down the potato salad.

"Declan, could you please get another table setting and some wine from inside?"

He abandoned the grill with relief, offering Rosie a grateful but subdued smile as he headed for the house. She wasn't sure what this conversation was about to entail, but at least now Declan and Maggie wouldn't interrupt before Tammy had the chance to pour out the details.

"Why don't you have a seat?" Rosie gestured to the table, "and I'll pour us some lemonade," she suggested.

A light breeze picked up in the very tops of the trees, sending the woods into a gentle cascade of whispers that chased away the stillness in the air. One of the boys let out a snort of laughter at something one of his buddies had said, and a bird called across the lawn to its mate. Rosie glanced up as she poured the drinks, feeling the pressure of her own energy melting away. She looked over at Tammy, searching for a sign that the other woman had picked up on the subtle magic that had just happened right in front of her.

She didn't seem to have noticed and had settled herself at the table, swiping at the tears now streaking down her face. The glass of lemonade being sat before her seemed to give her the confidence she needed to carry through with the story.

"I'm so sorry to barge in on y'all like this," she sniffled, "but I didn't know where else to go. You were so kind the day we all came out here. And I could use a little of your courage."

Her gaze jumped to the teenagers currently slinging pale yellow paint at each other as they painted Rosie's cabin, a punishment imposed after they had egged her and her daughter when they first came to Mosswood. Rosie glanced over at them, too, and had a feeling it was one of the teens' mothers, Priscilla Bishop, Tammy was really thinking of.

"You don't need to apologize," Rosie told her, taking a seat beside her at the picnic table Declan had built. "So let's get that out of the way right now. We're just having a cook-out, and you're officially invited."

Rosie's acceptance of Tammy sparked a chain reaction inside of her. It started as a small, warm tingle in her heart that radiated outwards, gathering more heat as it went. In no time at all it felt like it covered her entire body. Try though she might to hold it in, Rosie could feel her control starting to slip. The sensation of magic beginning to leak from her body was enough to incite a spike of panic; she couldn't risk showing her powers in front of Tammy and a bunch of local teenagers.

But the spike was enough of a hiccup to open up a bigger release. Energy spouted out of Rosie and up into the sky, making the leaves of the trees shudder as it dissipated into the atmosphere. But what goes up, as the saying went, must come down. The magic drifted back to the earth like snowflakes; shimmering energy that was only just barely visible to Rosie as she squinted at it. It settled like a comforter across the lawn, sending out an aura of approval that Rosie felt through to her very core. She thought back to what Declan had said, that night on the porch when he had informed her that she was the Queen of the Lost.

Was this what it felt like, to be taking steps forward into accepting that mantle?

Tammy finished wiping her eyes and offered a weak smile in return. "Thank you."

Rosie smiled back. "You're welcome. Now," she added, leaning towards Tammy with a soft expression. "Why don't you tell me all about it?"

Tammy nodded slowly and looked down at her hands clasped in her lap.

"Well. I went to the Church to drop off a batch of cookies I'd made for Sunday School," she began. "I came into the kitchen through the side door, so I guess he didn't hear me. The pantry door was open, and when I poked my head around in to see if anyone was inside, there he was with his pants around his ankles." She rolled her eyes toward Rosie. "I'd know his pasty butt anywhere."

Tammy looked up and down the ridge toward Mosswood. "In a town this small, you hear things."

Rosie smiled wryly. "Ain't that the truth."

Tammy laughed through the remnants of her tears, but then shook her head. "I've been hearin' for years about Terry runnin' around behind my back. But anytime I confronted him, he denied it. And I believed him. But seeing him with someone else, I knew all the rumors were true, and had been all this time."

Her tears ran anew, and Rosie pulled the apron from around her waist and handed it to her to use as a handkerchief. Tammy took it gratefully and wiped her eyes as she continued. "He followed me home, but I couldn't listen to him." She glanced at the laundry bag next to her on the table. "I just grabbed whatever I could reach and jumped in the car. Almost slammed his hand in the door."

Rosie interjected. "No more than he deserved."

She looked up at Rosie as though remembering herself and shook her head. "I can't believe how nice you're being. That day I saw you and Terry—"

Rosie interrupted. "That was all on Terry."

"—which I know now!" Tammy said. "I knew it the

minute we got home. He made all the same excuses then as he did today, so I knew he'd been lying then, too." She looked up at Rosie. "I'm sorry."

"Don't be," Rosie breathed. "None of this is your fault."

"I know," Tammy agreed more forcefully than Rosie would have suspected the softly spoken woman capable of. "I don't know whether I'm more sad or angry or just happy to be rid of him, but I do know that."

Rosie nodded knowingly. She remembered how she had felt when she'd reached the last straw with Randy and finally decided she was leaving him. It was like the last rubber band he had placed around her heart had snapped, letting the circulation back in. She reached out to place her hand on top of Tammy's and inspected her face.

"Can I offer you a little advice from someone who recently left her husband?"

"Please!" Tammy cried, dabbing at her eyes. "I don't know what to do with myself now."

"I know it's hard to let go of everything you'd hoped the relationship would be," she said, squeezing Tammy's hand. "But looking back is no way to move forward. From now on, things aren't *about* Terry anymore. They're about you."

Tammy looked up into Rosie's face. "I married Terry straight out of high school. I don't even know who I am except his wife."

Rosie dipped her head to one side, fixing Tammy

with an appraising look before she slapped a hand on the table. "No time like the present to find out."

She stood, hoping her momentum of activity would transfer into Tammy and distract her from the shock she'd had. She planted her hands energetically on her hips, like Wonder Woman. "Now. Why don't you put your things inside and help me finish the side salad?"

Tammy looked at the cabin and then back at Rosie. "Oh, no. I couldn't! You've got enough on your plate without takin' me in."

Rosie leaned forward to take Tammy's hand in both of hers, looking into the other woman's doe-like eyes. "You can and you will. Now's no time to be alone, Tammy." She patted Tammy's hand. "You should be with friends."

Tammy's eyes welled up with tears again, and she squeezed Rosie's hands. But the transferring of energy seemed to work, because she stood up from the picnic table and grabbed her bag of laundry in front of her. She took a deep breath.

"Okay," she said, more determinedly than seemed appropriate for the next line out of her mouth, "Take me to the lettuce."

Rosie smiled encouragingly.

The breeze kicked up a notch as she followed Tammy to the front porch. The lawn, which was almost due for mowing, rippled under the movement. As she followed Tammy up the porch steps, Rosie felt a pair of eyes on her. She turned to look at young Matthew Bishop, who was staring so hard at the pair of them that she thought he might have been trying to turn them to stone. Rosie felt a fierce protectiveness of Tammy well up inside of her. She lifted her chin by way of a silent challenge, and Matthew leaned down to dip his paint brush into his bucket again.

Her plan worked, and Tammy busied herself in the kitchen. Maggie resurfaced just in time to be given the job of setting the table, and Rosie stepped over to check that Declan wasn't burning the steaks.

"Everything okay?" he asked in a low voice, glancing up at her with a put-on smile that was entirely for Maggie's benefit.

Rosie peered at the meat. "It will be. Just needs a little time. I think you're done."

Declan pressed the steaks one more time with the barbecue tongs and then nodded. "Yep. Perfectly cooked."

"Only if you like eating charcoal," Rosie teased him. She skipped two steps ahead of him as he tried to pinch her with the tongs. A little thrill fluttered inside her as she thought about the plans she'd had for the evening, though their new house guest might have put a damper on things. She turned to look at Declan.

He looked sexy as all get-out. Grilling was such a simple task, but one that made him seem capable, determined, and a good provider all at once. The look of concentration on his rugged features was enough to give Rosie a glimpse of what he might look like focusing on other things, and she almost blushed before swatting the thought away.

They had only known each other a few weeks, but she felt an undeniable connection with him. Finding love had been the last thing on her mind when she'd decided to leave Randy. She had Maggie to think about, and her need to get them settled into a healthy and happy lifestyle trumped everything else. But Declan had shown that he wanted those things, too.

And it didn't hurt that Declan's arm muscles bunched and stretched as he turned the meat, or that the next best thing to him facing her was her getting to look at his taut, cargo-short-clad backside uninterrupted.

Well. Almost uninterrupted.

"Gross," Maggie complained from the table, and Rosie laughed lightly. Maggie glanced at Declan, who was transferring the meat from the grill to a plate. "You're *flirting* with him."

Rosie made brief eye contact with Declan and took a deep breath. Since she started school in Mosswood, Maggie's feelings toward Declan seemed to shift and change with the weather. Rosie didn't know whether it was because kids at school talked, or that Maggie had good days with her father as a turtle, or something she or Declan did. She read the sole library book in all of Mosswood's tiny building on parenting through divorce, and it had no better advice than what she already planned to do: be gentle and kind as she sorted through her feelings, and talk if she wanted to talk.

Declan picked up the cue.

"Which steak is yours, Miss Magnolia?" he asked ceremoniously, lowering the plate for her to pick out her meat.

Afternoon stretched into a pale, star-speckled evening. The food was good, in that filling, home-style way. Everyone at the table ate more than they should but not as much as they'd have liked, and after the dishes had been cleared the three adults sat there with their drinks while Maggie chased after fireflies with an empty Mason jar.

"This is the life I want for myself," Tammy said wistfully. "Slow and quiet."

Declan and Rosie exchanged knowing smiles across the table.

The old lanterns Rosie had found in the garden shed had been filled with cheap white candles that lit the table just enough for Rosie to see the yearning on Tammy's face. The half-painted cottage just visible in the fading light behind them made a mockery of the deal Rosie had made with Prissy, and the Spanish moss in the Oak tree by the table reminded her of the night Declan's camper had gone up in a blaze.

Slow and quiet? *Yeah, right.*

"It might not be easy to start with," Rosie said, watching Maggie giggle and dance across the lawn with her jar, "but you'll get there. We can start by making you a bed on the floor in Maggie's room—"

"Couch's taken," Declan added with a smirk that was part amusement, part disappointment that made Tammy smile. His eyes found Rosie's and she noticed an unasked question lingering in his gaze. He'd been staying with them in the cottage for weeks now, and undoubtedly would have liked to have moved into the bedroom. She hadn't invited him yet, but her thoughts had certainly been leaning that way over the past few days. Rosie smiled at him coyly, before forcing herself to look away.

"—and then," Rosie continued, "We'll help you get back on your feet again. Whatever you might decide that means for you."

"Well, for one thing, I'll never get up early to pack a cooler for a hunting trip again!" She said, as though only just thinking of it. "His hunting stories were—" she hesitated, looking for the right word and then, finding it, she blurted it out. "—boring!" Tammy barked a disbelieving laugh and clapped her hands over her mouth, as though she couldn't believe she'd said something unkind about her husband. And then, now that the floodgate had been opened, it seemed unlikely it would ever close again.

"Boring, boring, boring. The football he likes to watch is boring. His taste in food is boring. I've been half bored to death these last fifteen years and I didn't even know it!"

"But not anymore!" Rosie said proudly. "You can choose things for yourself, now! What do you like to watch on TV? What do you like to eat? Those are the only decisions ahead of you now!"

Tammy shook her head slightly, awe filling her large blue eyes as she met Rosie's gaze. "Thank you, Rosie." She reached across the table to take Rosie's hand. "You've proven to me that there are still good people in this world willin' to help a fellow Christian in need."

Declan swallowed a mouthful of his lemonade too quickly, and started to cough, earning him a glare from Rosie.

"Don't you worry about a thing," she told Tammy, turning to face her and ignoring Declan's obvious amusement. "You'll be just fine, you wait and see."

The breeze from earlier continued to wash around them; a soothing wave of warm fragrant air that made Rosie think of sweet grass, bare feet, and laughter. Something she couldn't explain felt like it had fallen into place. As Rosie continued to watch Maggie, her eyes darting every so often to Declan and then across to Tammy, she realized that they were all right where they were meant to be.

The dreaminess of Rosie's thoughts was interrupted by the unmistakable sound of a car burning up the road towards the cottage. Rosie frowned and looked over at Declan before training her eyes on the flash of a vehicle on the road behind the trees. Before too long, a snowy white SUV pulled off the road and into full view on the lawn. Rosie let out a steady breath to keep her cool, but it wasn't going to work.

"Here's a little of that 'slow'n easy' you were wishin' for, Tammy," Declan murmured sarcastically, pushing himself up out of his chair.

Tammy leapt up as well. "I'll just clear some of these dishes," she said, rushing to gather anything on the table that was within arm's reach.

Rosie placed a calming hand on Tammy's. "You haven't done anything wrong," she reminded her. Tammy froze, clearly trying to decide whether to give in to fight or flight. She eventually gave Rosie one anxious nod.

Rosie narrowed her eyes as she watched Prissy hop out of the car, slamming the door behind her. "Can we help you?" Rosie asked bluntly, crossing her arms over her chest.

"I came to speak to Tammy," Prissy said tartly, tossing her blonde mane over her shoulder and putting a hand on her hip. "I heard she was here, instead of home where she oughta be."

"I didn't realize you were Tammy's keeper," Rosie interjected, earning her Prissy's attention. The blonde woman's eyes narrowed down to mean little slits, and her unspoken retort was that she was *everyone's* keeper.

"Maybe you'd do well to mind your own business, Rosie," she said, feigning sweetness. "I know you're still new in town but buttin' in on people's private troubles ain't really the way things work around here."

Rosie snorted, amused. "And yet here you are," she laughed in disbelief.

"It's okay, Rosie." She turned to see Tammy standing uncertainly on the porch.

Prissy looked smugly over at Rosie as though she'd won a major victory. "A little privacy, please?" she said more than asked.

"She can stay," Tammy interjected. She looked up and met Rosie's gaze. "I want her to stay."

Prissy frowned so hard that Rosie thought she was looking for a way to earn her Botox top-up. She turned away from Rosie to cut her out of the conversation and focused on Tammy instead.

"I'm surprised you didn't come to me and Myles the *minute* you felt you were in crisis," she scolded.

"I just needed to get away from there," Tammy said, rushing on when she heard a disapproving cluck from

Prissy, "—and I knew that you would just try and talk me into staying."

"Honey, you know this ain't nothin' but a blip!" Prissy moved around to sit on the porch steps beside Tammy so that she wouldn't be able to look to Rosie for support. "Remember how it was when Terry asked you to Prom? And we all thought that God's plan for you was takin' shape at last, on account of how handsome he was, and how sweet, and how driven to have his own shop?"

"I remember," Tammy said, and Rosie could tell by her voice that she was fighting back tears again.

"Well, you can't be spittin' on God's plan!" Fire sparked in Prissy's voice, and she seemed to warm to her subject. "You *have* to forgive him. Married's married - for better or worse!"

Rosie felt her body cool and prickle all over with goosebumps. She remembered the minister saying those fateful words on *her* wedding day, and if they hadn't played over and over in her mind for years then she might have been strong enough to seek her and Maggie's emancipation from Randy sooner. She bristled and turned around in a rush. Tammy and Prissy both turned to look up at her; Tammy in admiration and Prissy in shock.

"You listen to me, Prissy Bishop," Rosie said in a low voice. "When someone stays in a marriage for 'better or worse', it's usually for the worse! Tammy has every right to feel how she's feeling! She caught her husband with another woman, after years of suspecting it!" With a fierce glare, Rosie walked up on the porch and wrapped an arm around Tammy's shoulder. "Instead of comin' out here to preach to her about forgiveness, why don't you go and preach to Terry about fidelity!"

Prissy gasped loudly again, drawing the attention of Declan and the teenagers who had been cleaning up their painting tools. She stood, clutching her car keys in her manicured claws. "I'm leavin'," she said darkly, "and I'm takin' the boys with me! I don't want them picking up any wrong ideas from being around a household like this one."

"Best news I've heard all day," Rosie told her cheerfully.

The boys didn't need to be told to down tools twice. They piled into Prissy's car like the Israelites following Moses. The car took off as soon as the last door was closed, leaving them all staring at it as it vanished back down the road. Rosie gave Tammy's shoulders a gentle squeeze just as another car pulled up.

Rosie's boss, Ben, got out of the old-but-tidy sedan and gave them a perfunctory wave as he went around to the trunk to fetch out a box.

"Ben!" Maggie's excited voice cut through the night. Rosie winced and then heard the colliding of bodies as Maggie ran full speed into a hug. Ben grunted from the impact, and then Maggie's voice rang out again. "Cool! I wanna sleep on the floor!" A moment later Maggie came dashing up the porch steps with a small black air pump and an electrical cord. Ben followed after at a Mosswood Mosey.

"Why was Prissy Bishop drivin' down the road lookin' madder than a cut snake?" he asked, a smirk hovering at the edges of his lips.

"Beats me," Rosie said, squinting into the darkness at him as he approached. "That woman does a lot of things I can't make any sense of."

"Fair enough," Ben grinned, stopping in front of Declan and holding out the box he was carrying.

"One inflatable camping mattress, as per your order. Hi Tammy," he added kindly.

Tammy looked from Ben to the mattress and back to Rosie, who shook her head.

"This one's all Declan," she said, giving Tammy one more light squeeze before releasing her.

"Thank you, Ben," Tammy said, "and you, Declan." Though the light was fading and it was getting harder to see, the emotion was clear in her voice.

"Thank me once we've actually managed to get it set up," Declan smiled.

"I'll give you a hand," Ben offered.

"And I'll fix us all a drink," Rosie added.

"Sure could use one," Ben admitted, at the exact same time as Tammy said "Oh, yes please!" Everyone smiled, and a gentle hum of laughter carried them up the porch steps and into the cottage. Rosie hung back, collecting the last few things off the table and rolling up the tablecloth. She followed, and even though her heart was full she wasn't sure it was going to be smooth sailing.

Maybe they were all where they were meant to be, but that didn't mean the world wasn't going to try to shift them out of place.

# CHAPTER TWO

Fox Cottage was quiet and still that night, in all rooms except her own, Rosie imagined. No matter how she tried to put it out of her mind, she kept coming back to the plan she had made that morning. Tonight was supposed to be The Night with Declan. But with everything else that had happened that day, and with another house guest who might overhear, the plan had fallen by the wayside.

That didn't keep her mind from wandering there every time she tried to turn it off and fall asleep.

She sat up in bed with a sigh and looked across the room to the standing mirror that had come with the cottage. She silently stepped out of bed and moved to stand in front of it in her night gown. It wasn't like she had youth on her side. She was thin but had plenty of imperfections and she was intimately acquainted with each of them. The puffy red stretchmarks on her belly, courtesy of motherhood. The pudgy donut-shaped flesh around her naval, that wouldn't shift no matter how many sit-ups she did. The less-than-perky bosom that had been waging war with gravity for the last twenty-five years. She knew them all, but she wasn't sure she wanted Declan to.

Her head swam with anxious thoughts. What if she didn't do it right? What if *he* didn't? What if he was too big, or what if she was? She'd had a baby. Did it just shrink back up after that? What if she was so unappealing, he couldn't even get it up? What if—*no*.

Rosie gripped the edge of the bed on each side of her. Thinking about all the what-ifs was doing her no good. It wasn't as though she had arrived at this decision lightly. Declan had been amazing with her and Maggie. When they kissed she felt an honest-to-goodness zing, as though something in her recognized something in him. It was the memory of the zing that got her onto her feet. The only way to go through with this was to stop overthinking it and just rip off the Band Aid already.

Rosie padded across the hallway on soft bare feet, slipping into the living room. Declan was standing by the window wearing nothing but his cargo shorts, looking out into the dark woods beyond the yard. A single candle glowed on the mantlepiece. He glanced over his shoulder at Rosie as she entered the room, and then his mouth fell open. His eyes met hers, then dropped to her lips, then kept falling down to her night gown and all the imperfections she had been so worried about. She saw his Adam's apple bob beneath his skin.

She walked towards him, slow and purposeful, and feeling more serene now than she had all day. She wanted him. That knowledge gave her all the courage she needed, and then some. When she reached him, she slid a hand up his neck to grasp his hair, drawing him down for a kiss.

If he was hesitant then he didn't show it, angling his head to deepen the kiss. His clipped beard grazed her cheek as he turned to face her, maneuvering his form to fit hers better. His hands slipped around her waist and before she knew it Rosie had lost herself.

Declan made a small growling sound in his throat and splayed his fingers against her back. She returned the eagerness of his kiss, and she could feel the intensity rising with each passing second. They shifted across the room, Rosie walking backwards until she felt the couch snug against the back of her legs and Declan's hard, insistent bulge pressed against her belly. Boldly, she dipped her tongue further into his mouth as she reached down to stroke him through his shorts.

His small growl almost became a roar.

She broke their kiss, her head snapping to the living room doorway as though she expected to get caught by Maggie, or Tammy, or both. Declan followed her gaze and then reclaimed her attention by nuzzling her neck.

"Jesus, Rosie," he murmured, trailing hot kisses all the way down to her collarbone. "You have no idea how badly I want you... how much I've wanted you this whole bloody time." He punctuated his admission by capturing her in another kiss.

He wanted *her*.

It was a revelation, and one that filled her with conflicting emotions. The part of her who wanted to be desired kissed him back, and for a few moments she was able to push everything else aside. She bathed in sensation; his touch, her lips tingling, his hands grasping her hips almost desperately, her fingertips exploring him.

She used her grip to pull him onto the couch, leveraging her body weight so they both tumbled onto the soft, floral-patterned surface. It wasn't wide enough for the both of them though, and Declan slipped backwards until he tumbled to the floor with an 'oof!' and a thud.

"Are you okay?" Rosie asked, peering over the edge of the couch until she could see that he was grinning up at her.

"Are you kidding?" he murmured, reaching up to stroke her cheek. "I've never been better. Now c'mere!" He snaked his hand around the back of her neck to cradle her head and sat up slightly. His other arm slipped around her waist, and deftly pulled Rosie off the couch to lay on top of him.

"Oh!" she exclaimed breathily before a slow smile crept onto her face. The candlelight to played across his face, and she suddenly felt more confident in her endeavor. Brazen, even. She leaned forward and began to kiss him again.

A soft giggle escaped her as he grunted with frustration, and she moved to sit up in between each meeting of their lips, coaxing him to sit up, too. She felt his shoe brush up against her ankle, but then paused in the middle of their kiss because, no, his shoe *hadn't* brushed up against her ankle, because he wasn't wearing shoes!

"What the—Ah!—*FUCK!*" Declan bellowed, and Rosie leapt to her feet in case her weight had been too much for him and his lower back had seized or something.

"Ohmygod!" she squeaked, "are you okay?" And then she looked down and squealed again.

The-turtle-formerly-known-as-her-ex-husband was attached to Declan's balls, or what she imagined was his balls, given he was still clothed. Declan writhed in agony, red-faced and grunting and unable to answer her or— apparently—dislodge Randy from having his jaws clamped down on Declan's nether regions. She stared as she tried to work out the logistics of it, and then she decided she'd better do what she could to help before Declan woke the whole house.

She got one hand on either side of the creature's shell, which was no mean feat given Declan's death throes. She gave an experimental tug, hoping to surprise the turtle into letting go.

"Argh!" Declan cried. "*Let-go-let-go-let-go!*"

Rosie lifted both hands in the air helplessly, wanting to help but terrified of making matters worse. But Fate, as it turned out, was plenty capable of doing that itself.

"What in the good Lord's name is goin' on in here?" Tammy gasped, skittering into the doorway with Maggie hiding behind her. And then her eyes fell from Declan's screwed-up face, down to the attack-mode turtle. "Oh *my*..." she breathed, her eyes wide. "I'll call 9-1-1!"

"No!" Declan cried, "don't!"

Maggie stepped out from behind Tammy, and marched forward with her hands on her hips. "Bad turtle! *Bad!* Let go right now!" She glared at the reptile fiercely.

All three grown-ups were looking at her aghast, and the turtle looked up at her with his beady little eyes. But surely enough, after holding on for just a few seconds longer, he released his grip. Declan gasped with relief and rolled into the fetal position, hands clasped protectively over his manhood. Rosie moved to his side, trying to see whether there was any blood, and Tammy hovered in the door to the living room.

Maggie grabbed up Randy and took him to his tank before scurrying back to the living room.

When Rosie was sure that Declan wouldn't bleed to death on her living room floor, she grabbed a hand towel and a packet of frozen peas from the kitchen, holding both out to Declan as she came back into the living room.

"Here," she said, handing over the makeshift ice pack. She turned to Maggie, her brows pulled together in disappointment and her heart still racing. "This is your final warning to keep that thing in its tank, Magnolia. Am I clear?"

Maggie looked down at the floor. "Yes ma'am." She pressed her lips together, and Rosie thought she could hear tears in her daughter's voice. "I'm real sorry, Declan."

Declan's only response was a strained noise that sounded something like 'uh-huh.'

Rosie bit back a sigh. "Tammy, would you please do me a favor and get Maggie back into bed?"

"Sure thing," Tammy said, "but if you need me, just holler, alright?"

Rosie nodded. With one last glance back at Declan, Tammy disappeared after Maggie down the hall.

Rosie moved back to Declan's side, bending down to try and further assess the damage.

"Just give me a minute," he grunted, shuffling along the floor until he could lift himself up onto the couch, "and we can start where we left off."

But the bravado Rosie had felt had vanished into thin air. She was back to feeling unsure about the situation, and she took the opportunity when it was presented to her. "You know what," she said, giving a little nonchalant shrug as if to say 'no biggie'. "We can wait and do this another time." She paused for a second but was too scared to give him the chance to fill the silence.

"Do you have everything you need for tonight?"

He looked surprised, and then disappointed. He glanced down as he applied the ice pack, and winced. "Pretty sure I'm all set."

"Goodnight then," she said, turning for her room.

"Goodnight, Rosie," he replied, talking to her retreating form.

# CHAPTER THREE

Rosie woke the next morning to the tell-tale smell of bacon and eggs cooking. She rolled out of bed with a smile on her face, thinking that if Tammy was going to cook breakfast and be helpful in the kitchen then she could stay just as long as she liked. By the time she padded into the kitchen barefoot, though, she could see that it was Declan and not Tammy who was frying up a storm.

"Smells great," she sighed, and her stomach grumbled in agreement. "Need a hand?"

"I've got it all under control, darlin'," Declan said, flipping eggs before crossing the kitchen to pour her a glass of juice. His hair was swept back from his face, lending him a more serious expression than the one he usually wore. He wore the cargo shorts and polo shirt he usually wore to work and had the dish cloth draped over his broad shoulder. Rosie arched a brow at him, taking a seat at the counter.

"You don't work on Sundays," she noted, watching him as he finished brewing the coffee. "What gives?"

He turned his back to her, leaving the coffee to sit a little longer in the pot while he checked the bacon. "I have to... get some stuff from Huntsville. Stock. For Elladine at The Moon."

Rosie's elevated brow became a frown, and she tilted her head to one side as he popped bread in the toaster. "But Sunday is one of the busiest days for the Moon Café," she said, suspicion coloring her tone. "Elladine's not gonna have time to worry about deliveries when she's up to her armpits in ravenous church-goers!"

"Guess they need the stock pretty bad," was all he said in reply. He took out three plates and began to serve up a delicious, greasy breakfast feast.

"Guess Tammy's at church already," Rosie mused, glancing at the clock and reaching eagerly for the coffee Declan placed next to her juice. "Thanks."

"I'm not goin' to Church today," a small voice announced. Tammy emerged like some kind of overly-organized butterfly from the cocoon of the hallway - hair done, subtle makeup applied, outfit on-point. Rosie and Declan both looked up at her.

"Fair enough," Rosie said before turning to Declan. "Looks like we need another plate."

"I'm not joinin' ya," he said, buttering toast and

distributing it between the plates while Tammy helped herself to some coffee. He glanced at the clock again, even though he had only just looked at it. "Gotta get—"

"—to Huntsville." Rosie completed for him, raising a brow. "Yeah, so you said."

He shrugged offering her a tight smile before placing two plates on the counter and popping the third in the oven to keep warm.

"You didn't have to get up and do all this if you needed to be elsewhere," Rosie said, unable to keep the huffiness out of her voice. As lovely as it was to have a magnificent breakfast cooked for her instead of by her, she wished he hadn't bothered at all if he had to rush out of the door and wasn't able to sit down and enjoy it too.

"It's nothin', love," he said, stepping around the counter. His smile then was more genuine, reaching his eyes and making their corners crinkle with that signature cheek she had come to associate with him. "You can show ya appreciation by doin' the dishes."

"The hell I will," Rosie countered, around a mouthful of hot buttered toast that she swallowed hastily. The cardinal rule of one person cooking and the other person cleaning had only worked in the past when she had been the one doing the cooking. When it became clear that he needed to use every dish in the house to cook one simple meal, Rosie had decided that he needed to learn to be more economical or wash his own dishes. "You made the mess, you get to clean it up. It'll be waitin' for you later."

"I'll look forward to it," he called back, laughter evident in his voice as he stepped out of the door.

"Some nerve," Rosie smirked into her coffee cup, glancing at Tammy who was still quiet. She took another bite of toast for the road and decided to wake Maggie up for her breakfast to give Tammy a few minutes to herself.

"And then we just dump in all that mayonnaise," Tammy cooed, lifting the bowl so that Maggie could scrape the creamy condiment into what looked like a perfectly legitimate chocolate cake— right up until then. The mayo fell in with a thick 'plop!' that seemed to satisfy Tammy.

"Go on then! Give it a good stir," she told Maggie, who didn't need to be asked twice.

"How come it don't taste like mayo once it's all cooked?" Maggie asked, mixing with gusto.

"Oh, it's just a little magic!" Tammy said, throwing Rosie a conspiratorial wink.

Maggie brightened, missing the wink as she straightened her back and glanced at her mom with wide eyes. "Really?!"

Rosie gave her daughter a fleeting look, shaking her head ever so slightly. Maggie deflated and went back to her mundane mixing, but Tammy was on a roll.

"Once we're done with the cake and it's cooling, I'll show you how to mix up the frosting."

"My favorite part," Rosie announced dreamily, making Tammy and Maggie both grin in anticipation.

Tammy tipped the cake batter into the tin banged it on the counter twice to release any air bubbles and then put it in the oven. Maggie turned to Rosie as soon as nothing more interesting was happening.

"Can I go outside while it bakes, Mom?"

Rosie nodded, silently thanking her lucky stars that her daughter actually enjoyed exercise and the outdoors. Of course it might have had something to do with the fact they couldn't afford iPads.

She watched Maggie dash outside, wrapping one arm around her stomach and placing the other hand on her hip. Tammy fell silent, and when Rosie glanced back at her she was collecting up the dirty baking dishes wearing that same somber expression she'd had on her face earlier.

"It must be time for a caffeine hit!" Rosie exclaimed, popping some on to brew while Tammy busied herself with the dishes at the sink. Rosie watched her swirling them under the hot water, adding dish soap, grabbing the dish cloth.

It was a ritual she had performed so many times herself that she knew it like the back of her hand, but seeing another woman carrying it out reminded her of how alike they all were. One woman's troubles could easily be another's. At least when she had left Randy she had come to a new town, away from anyone whose opinion she might have cared about. Poor Tammy was stuck in her one-horse hometown, and already wasn't attending a Church she loved on account of wagging tongues.

Rosie shifted backwards toward the counter and hoisted herself up onto it. It was a habit that neither foster homes nor Randy had been able to break her of. She crossed her legs at the ankles and let them swing gently. The smell of coffee soon filled the small but cozy kitchen.

"It took me years to realize how unhappy I was with my ex," she said slowly, measuring her words so that she could try and make sure they came out the way she intended them to. Tammy looked up, suds covering her hands and interest sparked behind her eyes.

"I dunno why," Rosie continued, shrugging and looking up at the streaky paint of the ceiling. "He was cruel, and selfish, and not at all who he'd pretended to be, in the beginning. But I think there was something in me that needed to be needed, and I mistook his controlling nature for protectiveness."

"That sounds just like Terry," Tammy sighed, and Rosie was so relieved that the other woman was following her lead that she could have beamed at her. "Any time I wanted to spend more time volunteering at Church or helping at the school, he would just tell me that I needed to 'stop givin' the best parts of myself to folk who don't appreciate it'." She sighed. "Maybe if I wasn't always doing things for others, he wouldn't have strayed the way he did."

"No," Rosie said gently, placing a comforting hand on Tammy's shoulder. "You're not to blame for his unfaithfulness. That's on him."

"Is it?" Tammy asked, looking up. "He was always on at me to take better care of myself, and to make more of an effort in the bedroom. And now it seems like everyone's quick to remind me to honor my marriage vows and forgive him that I feel like a bad Christian because I don't *want* to forgive him at all."

Rosie nodded slowly. "I can understand how it might feel like somehow you caused Terry's eye to wander, because I went through those same feelings when Randy would take to another woman's bed," she told Tammy. "But men like him and Terry will always want whatever it is that they don't have at the time. And they'll spend their whole lives looking for it, and end up with nothing to show for it." She bent to better look more directly into Tammy's face. "And I won't insult you by pretending that I have all the answers, 'cause I don't. I'm not a good Christian, and I don't know what it's like for you to be under that kind of pressure. All I do know is that if there's any sinning to be pointed at, it's Terry's."

"I hope you're right," Tammy said. She looked so sad, so different to the decent, friendly person Rosie had first met. Now she looked defeated and bitter, and the change was so pronounced that Rosie's heart ached for her. "Can you believe that we've been trying for a baby? I thought that if we had a child, his attention might not stray so far," Tammy added in a small voice. "I'm ashamed to admit it, now. I was stupid to think any of that could fix—"

"Hey!" Rosie interrupted her, shaking her head strongly. "You wanted a family and a happy marriage. There's nothin' stupid about that. Stupid is your husband not knowing how good he's got it."

A knock on the door made both women jump.

"It better not be Terry!" were the next words out of Tammy's mouth. A stern frown had taken up residence on her forehead, and she looked ready to give him a piece of her mind if it was.

"It's not," Rosie said, although she wasn't entirely sure that it wasn't. "I'll get it, and you make the coffee."

Upon opening it, she got a shock to see Pastor Bishop standing on her doorstep. Knowing his horrible wife and son hadn't made for a favorable impression of him in Rosie's mind, but when she drank in the sincere and concerned expression on his face and the small shopping bag he held in his hands, she hoped he was about to prove her wrong.

"Hi there," he said with a calm smile. His dark hair had been combed into a less ostentatious version of Elvis Presley's pompadour. Rosie forgave him for the fussiness of the style (and for the gaucheness of adopting it when his wife's name was Priscilla) when she saw that it set off his pale blue eyes brilliantly. "I'm Pastor Myles Bishop. You must be Miss Rosemary Bell." He stuck out a hand.

"I am indeed," she replied, fixing him with a warm smile and shaking his hand. Nice firm shake. She approved. "It's nice to meet you, Pastor Bishop."

"Myles, please!" he chuckled lightly. "Any friend of Tammy Holt's is a friend of mine."

Aha. So that was the reason for the visit. Tammy hadn't shown up at Church for the day, and so they had sent down the Big Guns to bring the wayward sheep back to the flock. Figured. Rosie kept her smile in place, but it was a little more measured now.

"What can I do for you?" she asked.

He had the grace to look sheepish. "Well, Miss Rosemary, I noticed that Tammy's shining light was missin' from our congregation this mornin'. I know that she's had a rough couple days. I thought I would duck out between my obligations just to let her know she's bein' thought of."

Rosie softened. Even if he had been sent there by his wife in an attempt to win Tammy over, Rosie knew it would mean a lot to Tammy to have him stop by. "Would you like to come in?" she asked him. "Tammy's in the kitchen."

"Well, now that I don't doubt," he smiled, allowing

himself to be led through the hall. "Tammy's the best cook in all of Mosswood!"

When Rosie entered the kitchen ahead of their impromptu guest, it was clear she had heard the praise. Tammy's round cheeks were flushed, and she had tried to hastily brush errant streaks of flour off her dress.

"Pastor Bishop!" she squeaked. "What're you doin' here? The senior luncheon should be startin' right about now."

"Oh, I had Leanne fill in for me today," he announced, setting the shopping bag gently on the kitchen counter. He levelled Tammy with a gentle smile, dipping his head so that he could peer into her face as though trying to make an assessment. Whatever he saw in her eyes must have satisfied him, because he straightened again.

"I had an important delivery to make that couldn't wait," he told her, reaching into the bag. He pulled out a tub of Ben & Jerry's and a simple black Bible with some pages in it marked with post-it notes. Tammy gasped with surprise. He smiled but shrugged a shoulder wryly. "By the look of that divine cake, I can see that you're all set for comfort food. The ice cream'll keep. Reckon you will, too."

"Thank you, Pastor," Tammy gushed. She shifted her weight from one foot to the other, doing a subtle little dance that betrayed the fact that she didn't know how else to thank him.

"You can thank me by takin' care of yourself," he

told her. "Don't you rush to come back to Church before you're ready. We'll wait for you." He turned to Rosie then, his smile widening. "And thank you, for lookin' out for Tammy just when she needs a friend the most."

"I wouldn't have it any other way," Rosie told him, and she meant it.

# CHAPTER FOUR

"**R**oot beer, actual beer, OJ," Rosie said, handing the drinks out around the tiny kitchen table before sitting down with her own sweet tea. Declan worked at shuffling a deck of cards, but he kept dropping some out of the pack.

"You're not holding them right," Maggie counselled him, taking a sip of her OJ. "You gotta cradle them in your fingers. Don't hold on too tight."

Declan side-eyed her. "Do you think you can do better?"

"I *know* I can do better," Maggie grinned.

"Uh-uh," he told her, holding the cards out to her.

Maggie took them and turned them over in her hands as though adjusting her grip. Before Declan could roll his eyes, Maggie cut the cards with expert precision and began to shuffle them with all the grace of a casino dealer.

The bottom of Declan's beer bottle hit the table in disbelief, and he gaped at Maggie who was grinning and enjoying herself immensely. Tammy giggled, clapping good-naturedly.

"Where'd ya learn how to do that?" he breathed, watching Maggie's nimble hands at work as though mesmerized.

"My dad," Maggie said offhandedly.

"It's a useful skill," Declan told her with reverence, causing Rosie to raise a brow in his direction.

"Nope," she said having another sip of her drink.

Declan hunched down in his chair, but wisely didn't reply.

Maggie dealt four hands for Go Fish, and Rosie ignored Declan's muttered comment about thinking that game was a waste when Maggie was all set to deal Texas Hold 'Em.

"Left of Dealer starts," Maggie declared.

"Alright!" Tammy said, gathering up her hand and having a quick look through her cards before looking across the table at Rosie. "Any threes?"

Rosie checked her cards and slid one across the table to Tammy who wriggled like an excited puppy in her chair.

"Any tens?" she asked Declan. He pursed his lips and slid her a card.

"Maggie's not the only card shark at the table, I see," he muttered. "I'll be watchin' you lot!"

Tammy beamed and turned her attention to Maggie. "Got any eights?"

Maggie considered it for a few moments, and then shook her head theatrically. "Go fish!"

"She may not be the only card shark here," Rosie chuckled, "but she's the *best.*"

Declan groaned, just as his cell phone buzzed on the table. "Saved by the bell," he announced, standing up. "Sorry everyone, I'd better take this. Gimme ten?"

"Five," Maggie countered.

"Ah, you're ruthless!" He laughed as he passed her to step out into the garden.

Rosie glanced at the clock and then stood up. "I'm just gonna dash out and grab some herbs from the garden for dinner," she announced.

"Better to do it now than in the dark," Tammy agreed.

The warmth of the afternoon greeted her, as she stepped outside, and she moved towards the side of the cottage where her little herb garden grew under the eaves, next to the trellis holding the stumps of an old grapevine. She realized too late that it put her within eavesdropping distance of Declan on his phone call. She snipped off an herb with her sheers and tried not to listen, but Declan's tone was so different from usual that she found her attention drawn to the conversation anyway.

"I told ya I'm workin' on it," he hissed into the phone, his Irish accent thicker than usual, maybe because he sounded so short with whoever was on the other end of the line. She leaned back where she was stooped down, trying to see around the corner of the house to where he was standing. He was huddled by the dogwood hedge, hunched over and arms crossed tightly over his chest. He looked as tense as he sounded. She stood with the herbs in hand to wait for him to finish, so she could ask if he was alright.

"She's more stubborn than a mule, an' no mistake," he continued.

Supportive feeling gone. Was he talking about her? Her heart pounded in her chest as she tried to shake off the feeling, but the past leaves its mark on those who live it, and her husband used to speak ill of her within hearing distance all the time as a way to break her spirit.

But Declan wouldn't do that. She was sure of it. Absolutely certain.

"Yes, Da. I know. I *know*. I'll get rid of her. Yes," Declan sighed, sounding as though he was struggling to keep a tight rein on his temper, "I know it was my own stupid fault. Alright? Can you just trust me to take care of it?"

Rosie's courage and certainty faltered. She stepped around the corner of the house again, taking deep breaths to steady her pounding heart. Declan finished his conversation.

"Alright—bye now. Bye bye. Bye."

Rosie blinked at the weirdness of the goodbye and

then balked when she realized that Declan was heading her way to go back into the house. She scrambled for the nearest bush, and only just managed to pretend to be plucking sprigs from it as Declan rounded the corner.

His eyes widened when he saw her, and it was clear that he was worried she had overheard his conversation. "Oh!" he said, rubbing the back of his neck and slipping his phone quickly into his back pocket as though he thought it might give him away. "I thought you were inside, love."

She held up her handful of herbs by way of explanation. Declan lifted his head in acknowledgment. She inspected him.

"Everything alright?"

"Oh, yeah," he said, feigning casual indifference. "Just Becker—from Wood & Wax? They need me to pick up some stuff for them next week."

She didn't feel so bad for lying about overhearing him, now. "Great," she said.

"Better get back inside," he said then, obviously keen to escape the awkwardness of the situation. "Maggie only gave me five minutes' reprieve."

"See you in there," was all Rosie said in return. She listened to Declan's boots moving towards the porch, then taking the steps two at a time, then carrying on into the house. She stood there for a few more seconds before heading back inside herself.

Rosie thought that her days of having a tag-along at work were over once Maggie started school. But with the cottage as sparkling clean as Tammy could make it in the few days she had been staying with them there was little else for her to do, and keeping busy seemed to be Tammy's singular goal in life. She had once called Priscilla Bishop the busiest woman in Mosswood, but seeing how Tammy volunteered for every little thing, cooked every meal, cleaned every dust bunny, and did anything and everything to be useful, Rosie didn't think it possible that anyone was busier than her.

Ben hadn't said a word when the pair of them had turned up at the beginning of Rosie's shift. Rosie had to admit that it certainly made her shift pass more quickly and pleasantly. When a bedraggled-looking man wandered through the store's automatic doors ten minutes before her shift was due to finish, Rosie was almost walking on air - she'd actually had *fun* for the first time ever at work. She was so grateful for her job and the comfort it provided for herself and Maggie, but it wasn't her dream job.

"Hi there," she greeted the man, who glanced at a beat-up looking cab outside before grunting a hello and wandering down one of the aisles. *Out-of-Towner*, Rosie thought to herself, unable to stop the grin from spreading over her face when she realized how much of a local that thought made her feel. Mosswood (and a large portion of its residents) could be a real pain in the ass, but it was the only real home she'd ever known.

When the man eventually wandered back to the counter and filled it with the contents of the basket he had picked up somewhere along the way, Rosie began to scan his items and offered him a sympathetic smile. "Long day?"

"You have no idea," the man sighed, rubbing a hand over his eyes before reaching for his wallet. "Just drove all the way out here from Atlanta for a fare. Woman wouldn't stop bossing me around—change the radio station—turn it up—turn it down—don't take that turn —pull in here."

He rattled off the list of complaints in a high pitch, making a terrible attempt at an English accent. Rosie grinned and allowed herself a small chuckle. She knew all about irritating customers. Though thankfully these days, Prissy seemed to make an effort to come in when she wasn't serving, thank goodness.

"I was from Atlanta originally. It's a long drive," she told him, with a small smile. "But at least the drive back will be a quiet one!"

"You're damn right," he chuckled, and then he peered at her a little more closely. "Hey, I thought you looked familiar. You came out here from Atlanta a while back, right? You and a little girl - picked you up in the middle of the night? I was your driver that day."

"Wow," Rosie said, bagging up the man's

items. Panic flared within her, until she calmly reminded herself that Randy was now a turtle. "Good memory."

The man snorted. "It was one of the weirdest days of my life," he said, suddenly seeming a little agitated as he checked his watch. "and now a second fare to Mosswood. Maybe it's someone you know."

Rosie quirked a brow, wondering what on earth could be so weird about him driving them. "I hope not," Rosie joked lightly. "I didn't leave anyone behind in Atlanta that I'd care to keep in touch with."

"Can't say's I blame you," the cabbie said with a shudder. He placed the exact amount he owed on the counter and shook his head. "She don't seem like the type of person many people would wanna be mixed up with." And with that he gave his thanks, picked up his groceries, and hurried back to his cab.

Rosie frowned as she watched him go, a feeling of unease building inside of her like the swelling of a balloon getting ready to burst.

# CHAPTER FIVE

"**I** wish Declan was here to tuck me in tonight," Maggie complained as she crawled into her bed that night. "He promised to tell me the story about the Pooka."

Rosie blinked back a suspicious expression, because she, too, was wondering what mysterious circumstance had taken Declan away that evening. Something was eating at her, and she didn't know quite what. She smoothed the lavender colored bedspread over her daughter, as though it would smooth out her worries, too.

"What on earth's a Pooka?" she asked with a smile.

"I don't know," Maggie admitted, "he was going to tell me!"

"Maybe he'll tell you the story another night, Pumpkin. Have you got your water bottle in case you get thirsty in the night?"

"It fell under the bed." Maggie pulled an 'oops!' face. "Sorry."

"No biggie." Rosie slipped off the end of the bed and onto her hands and knees, groping around under the bed.

Her fingers closed on something, and it took her a moment to register it as scratchy and light, instead of smooth and full of water. She drew it out and held it up to the light so the she could see it, and then she threw it back down onto the floor immediately.

"What was that!?" Maggie asked, panic rising in her voice. "Was it a spider?"

The knotted-up straw looked nothing like a spider. The intricately wound loops and knots were reminiscent of something she had seen before. And then she saw a flat rock that had been broken in half, with straw woven through a number of holes in its smooth surface holding it somewhat together. Had she broken it when she threw it on the floor?

"It's nothing," Rosie lied, as she recalled the knots in the Celtic leather bracelet that Declan wore. "Just some fluff from something. Probably the rug." She snatched the item up and stuffed it into the band of her denim shorts, ignoring the hot, prickling sensation that rasped against the skin of her belly.

Magic.

She delved desperately under the bed, retrieving the water bottle and placing it on Maggie's bedside table.

Her mind was racing ahead with all the panic she had managed to talk Maggie out of.

"Thanks Mom."

"You're welcome Pumpkin. Sweet dreams."

"You, too. Love you."

Rosie held her breath, not wanting to let her anxiety show. The magic was starting to feel like a bad sunburn against her abdomen. "Love you, too," she said, before pressing a kiss to Maggie's forehead and forcing herself to walk out of the room as normally as she could manage.

Once she was halfway down the hall, she made a beeline into the washroom, closing and locking the door behind her. She ripped the woven straw out from under the clothing and threw it to the ground, lifting up the hem of her shirt to examine the large red welt it had left against her skin.

It was definitely magical.

It was definitely not friendly.

And it had definitely been left under her kid's bed by Declan.

Things were starting to add up in ways she could no longer simply pass off as coincidence. Declan's phone call with his dad. The messages and missed calls. The vanishing act he'd been pulling lately. Lies about helping Elladine at the Moon Café, or the ladies at Wood & Wax.

Rosie let her shirt fall back down and picked the strange straw knot up in a hand towel. The magic was dulled by the cloth surrounding it, but she could still feel it pulsing in her hand as she made her way to the living room.

Rosie barely slept. She had been trying to think of possible explanations for the strange talisman she had found under Maggie's bed. Her mind had finally exhausted itself somewhere in the early hours of the morning and she had fallen into a restless sleep, one ear listening out for the sound of Declan's key in the front door.

Any relief she felt at opening her bedroom curtains onto what seemed like a cooler day vanished when she realized that a fight with Declan was brewing. She wanted answers, and she was determined to get them. Rosie dressed quickly and made for the living room, but pulled up short when the couch was empty.

The shock of him not coming home bled through her morning. She got Maggie ready for school in a daze, dropped her off at the gate and started her morning shift at the Go-Go Mart. In between customers she Googled straw knots on her phone, but only came up with results for the squiggly kind that were only good for sipping milkshakes with.

Damn.

She was putting new receipt paper in the cash register when Ben emerged from his office with a stack of new Herald of Hope magazines from the Church. Rosie only just managed to resist rolling her eyes before an image of the cab driver from Atlanta popped into her mind.

"Ben?" she asked slowly, turning to face her boss. "Why'd you hire me?"

Ben blinked, turning to face her. His expression was a mixture of amusement and concern. "... because I needed someone to cover the shifts I couldn't?" he replied just as slowly, before breaking out into a smile. "Geez, Rosie, way to put a guy on the spot."

"Sorry. Didn't mean to." She pursed her lips, threading the paper through the feeder. "Just wanted to know what made you decide to take a chance on an Out-of-Towner is all," she lied. "I'm sure there were plenty of locals who would have jumped at the chance."

"You'd think so, huh?" Ben plopped the magazines on the counter, and then leaned against it. "But apparently not. You were my only applicant! Just goes to show Declan isn't always the sharpest tool in the shed."

Rosie frowned. "Declan?" What on earth did he have to do with this?

"Shortly after he started delivering here, he said that I worked too hard and that I oughta get someone who could help out." He smiled at her politely. "Seemed like a good idea at the time. But no one applied, except you.

And I'm sure glad you did. Place wouldn't be the same without you."

She glossed over his backtracking. "Who was your delivery driver before Declan?"

And then the strangest thing happened. Ben's eyes became glassy, and it was like for a split second he wasn't present in his own mind. A normal person might not have even noticed, but Rosie also felt the magical charge that pulsed in the air around them as the change took place. And then it was gone, and Ben was back to normal.

"D'you know, I can't rightly remember his name!" He rubbed the back of his neck and looked up at the ceiling, before looking back at Rosie. "Nope! Completely vanished from my brain. He wasn't very reliable, though. Not like Declan."

No, Rosie thought. Declan could definitely be relied upon... but for what?

She gave Ben a half-hearted smile to end the conversation, and then turned to begin sorting out the Herald of Hope copies he had left for her. That's when she noticed someone looking in through the large plate windows outside: an elegant, willowy woman wearing tan slacks, a white short-sleeved blouse and large sunglasses under an even larger wide-brimmed hat. She lifted a hand to pull down her shades for a moment, glanced at Rosie with bright hazel eyes, and then pushed the glasses back up her nose with a smirk. And then she continued down the sidewalk outside.

What on earth was going on?

The loading dock at the Go-Go Mart, as the unofficial break room, was the only place quiet enough to get a bit of peace. Rosie sat in the old armchair under the rickety porch with her phone held limply in her hand.

She had briefly thought about calling for reinforcements. At least if Tammy had come into the store they would have been able to gossip about what had happened and try to make sense of it. But the snowball effect of Declan's odd behavior and the strange circumstances around her arrival in Mosswood had become an avalanche by now, and even Tammy's stalwart cheerfulness and logic wouldn't be enough to put the brakes on it before it hit.

Even an icy cold can of soda wasn't enough to soothe her hectic thoughts. She let it rest on the arm of the chair, drawing a pattern in the condensation on the side as she watched a few errant brown leaves skittering along the lane. The first few signs of fall were all around them, and Rosie found herself longing for the cooler days. It was her favorite time of year, and even her personal struggles didn't prevent her from looking forward to it.

A familiar rumble at the end of the lane made her sit up straighter, and her mouth went dry as Declan's truck pulled up at the Go-Go Mart's loading dock. She had been going over what she wanted to say to him in her head for several days now, methodically adding each new thing to her growing pile of grievances. But as he jumped down from the truck and joined her on the dock, Rosie felt as though all of her arguments rushed forward like fans at a rock concert.

"Well, good morning gorgeous," he smiled. Rosie just stared. Usually she thought his smile looked genuine. It crinkled the corner of his sea-green eyes and made them sparkle with just the right amount of mischief. He had a tiny dimple in his right cheek, almost hidden by his neatly trimmed ginger beard. And he ambled toward her with a casual athleticism that usually made her both envious and admiring all at once.

But today she thought she saw a shadow in his eyes, his beard looked a little scraggly for her tastes, and his loping gait seemed more shifty than sexy.

He tilted his head, frowning slightly at her lack of response. "Or... not."

"Declan, what's going on?"

"What are you talking about?"

She wasn't fazed by his haughtiness. "I found your broken stone talisman under Maggie's bed."

He looked stricken, as though he had been slapped in the face. "Jesus, Rosie, I..."

"And I overheard your conversation on the phone the other day," she continued, looking into his eyes. His mouth fell open, but no other sound came out, so she continued. This time the words came more slowly, because to her this was the biggest crime of all, and she was hoping she was wrong.

"And I'm pretty sure you put a spell on Ben to make him hire me at the Go-Go Mart."

His fingertips gripped the bridge of his crooked nose. He let out a long sigh before responding.

"If the stone was broken, it meant that the spell worked. I wanted to make sure you were safe," he said with a chop of his hand, "That you and Maggie had the chance to start your new life."

She froze. "So what? You're saying you knew me before we even came here?" She felt her features go slack and realization dawned. "You put a spell on the cab driver to bring us here, didn't you?"

He nodded and she exhaled with force.

She glared at him. "What else? What else did you do?"

He looked her in the eye as though weighing whether to tell her everything or give her the CliffNotes version. And then he began.

"I..." His shoulders slumped as he shook his head and continued, "I made Carol-Ann rent you the cottage without a credit or background check. And then I..." He winced as though he knew the next part would be one Rosie wouldn't like, "Convinced Ben he needed an assistant, and made it so you were the only one who'd see the advertisement."

Rosie felt her heart drop into her stomach. Getting the job at the Go-Go Mart had been one of the things that really made her feel like she was making her own way in the world after leaving Randy. She'd known the cottage being vacant and ready to rent on such meager information as she could provide had been lucky, so she hadn't owned that accomplishment like a badge of pride. But her job? That had been hers, or so she thought; the first thing that was hers in a long time. And then thinking of that time when she first left Randy made a dark thought come to the front of her mind.

"Did you make me leave Randy?" She lifted her gaze and peered into Declan's face for any sign of dishonesty.

It was a loaded question and Rosie wasn't entirely sure that she wanted the answer. If he said yes, then it meant that all her courage and all the progress she had made towards creating a new life for Maggie and herself had been orchestrated by Declan. Was she about to learn that she never really had the strength to leave Randy after all?

He shook his head, stepping closer to her. "No," he said gently. "Of course not. Even if I had wanted to, I couldn't. Your bloodline is born from free will, Rosie. My power's not enough to override yours."

She was flooded with relief, but she chose not to show it. Instead, she let her indignance for the people around her shine through. "Shame that the same can't be said for the cab driver, and Carol-Ann, and Ben!"

Declan winced again. "I wanted you to be somewhere that was safe from Randy, where I could help you and keep an eye on you."

"You were protecting the prophecy, not us! You're no better than Randy, controlling my life and all the things around it for your own selfish reasons!"

Declan stood mutely on the loading dock, either not sure what to say or wisely choosing to hold his tongue. Rosie met his gaze.

"I trusted you," she sighed, tears starting to course down her cheeks. "With myself. With my daughter. And it's all been a lie?"

"The last thing I did was get Ben to hire you, Rosie. I swear." Declan blinked, looking for all the world as though he might have been close to crying himself.

"I wanted to make my own way!" Rosie shouted, her voice ringing out down the alley. She took a deep breath, and then lowered her volume. "I wanted to do it for myself, and for Maggie—but mostly to prove I was more than the nobody Randy said I was. And you took that away from me."

She turned away. She couldn't bear to look at him standing there with his sad eyes as though somehow he had a right be upset when it was his lies and manipulation that had landed them both in this to begin with. "I want you out of the cottage by the time I get home. I need to not be around you."

"But... what will you tell Maggie?" He asked. She wanted to punch him for even asking.

"I'll fix that part of your mess." Rosie lifted a hand to swipe the tears from her face. "If you had cared about how any of this would affect Maggie then you wouldn't have done it."

She didn't know how long he stood there, watching her watch the armchair she had just vacated. But a little while later, she heard him walk back across the dock and get into the truck. It rattled down the lane, and Rosie picked up her drink, ran her fingers through her bangs to sweep them out of the sweat on her forehead, and then went back to work.

# CHAPTER SIX

**B**y the time they came walking up the drive after school that day, Rosie still hadn't gathered the strength to tell Maggie that Declan wouldn't be at Fox Cottage when they got there. She was so distracted trying to come up with some explanation why his things wouldn't be there, she didn't notice the eight or so cars parked on her front lawn until Maggie mentioned it.

"Tammy's having a party," she said, sounding excited at the prospect. Rosie raised and brow and set her jaw. She would recognize Prissy's gaudy oversized SUV anywhere, and she was *not* in the mood. Rosie stepped past Maggie and pushed, bristling already, into the house, only to gape at the sight past the screen door.

Her living room had become an honest-to-goodness makeshift chapel for the Hand of God Southern Baptist Church.

Every chair in the house had been dragged into the room and placed in a circle, and each of those chairs was occupied by a member of the congregation. Tammy sat in one by the fireplace, looking miserable. And it was no wonder. Nobody in the room had seemed to notice the two of them come in, but then they were all too busy talking over one another that it was no wonder.

"We only want the best for you, hon," Leanne Coombes was saying, her face seeming more pinched than ever. "We wouldn't be doin' right by you if we didn't stop in to help you see the light."

"I just don't see how this *is* the light," Tammy replied, albeit meekly. "Terry's been makin' a fool of me for years."

"He's a fool himself, he's so in love with you," Prissy snapped from Rosie's large wicker armchair, the most throne-like chair in the house. She smoothed the heat out of her tone before adding, "Just like he oughta be. He just made a mistake's all."

"More than one!" Tammy grunted. A red-haired woman that Rosie didn't know put a hand on Tammy's shoulder.

"But you've made mistakes too," the woman said. "Just look at you. Skippin' out on Sunday Services. Ignoring Terry when he's tried to beg for your forgiveness."

"And just look at who you're relyin' on in your time of need," Prissy interjected, throwing up her hands to indicate their surroundings. "Puttin' your faith in *Rosie Bell?* Doesn't that show you just how far off God's path you really are?"

"I'd say it shows that she's on a better path than any of you," Rosie said, her voice clear and strong. "After all, *I'm* not trying to convince a woman to overlook an unfaithful husband." Almost a dozen pairs of eyes snapped to look at her.

"Well I wouldn't expect *you* to understand or appreciate the sanctity of marriage," Prissy huffed. "After all, you tried to tempt Terry your own self!"

"Rosie did no such thing," Tammy announced in a much louder voice that made everyone's gaze volley back to her.

Rosie gave her a terse but grateful nod. She was beyond angry.

"Just who do you all think you are, making yourselves at home in my house, upsetting my guest?" she asked, earning a few shame-faced glances from women she didn't know. "If Pastor Myles doesn't have any objections to Tammy needing space and privacy to deal with her martial issues—no matter the outcome—then I can't see how any of *you* have a right to be concerned!"

Prissy tossed her blonde mane over her shoulder. "My husband is *very* concerned," she said, standing. "We all are! We're such a close-knit congregation that one person's troubles belong to all of us."

"Funny," Rosie mused, tilting her head to one side.

"He didn't seem terribly concerned when he took time out of Church on Sunday afternoon to bring Tammy some of her favorite ice cream. That is, he *was* concerned—for Tammy's well-being, and not much else."

Prissy looked like she'd been slapped in the face. Had she not known about her husband's visit to Tammy? The color had drained from the other woman's face, and a tendon clenched and released in her jaw. "Don't you act like you know anything about my husband, Rosemary Bell!"

"I've had just about enough of this," Tammy said then. The room went quiet, and Tammy seemed to take that to mean that she had the floor. She stood up.

"Some of y'all are here because you have known Terry and me a long time," she began, wringing her hands together as she seemed to struggle to find the words she wanted to get out. "And I know you're worried about what this situation will mean for us, and for the Church, and for the community as a whole." She glanced at Leanne, who nodded just once and then looked down at the floor in resignation.

"But some of you are just here for the gossip, and that just makes me sick to my heart. Nobody knows what all goes on in a marriage behind closed doors, and every good time I had with Terry had its equal measure of—of..." she hesitated. She looked around the room as though someone would supply her with the right word.

Her blue eyes met Rosie's gray ones across the room, and a spark of courage grew between them.

Tammy pursed her lips, and then continued. "Of *sorrow*. No matter why you're here, y'all have got to give me some space. I plan on doin' right by myself for once. And I know that my true friends'll still be by my side after the dust settles."

Maggie stepped around until she was next to Tammy, and wrapped a small arm around her for a soothing hug. Rosie watched her daughter and then met Tammy's gaze, nodding a supportive nod.

"Now if y'all don't mind," Tammy called out, "We need to be gettin' on with our day."

The ladies began to file out of the house. One or two of them had the decency to stop by Rosie and apologize for the inconvenience, which she gracefully acknowledged with nods. She locked the door after the last one, watching Tammy and Maggie carrying the last of the chairs back to the dining table.

"I thought we could all use a Friday treat, so I prepped my famous fried chicken with all the trimmings." Tammy indicated a cloth-covered tray on the counter. "It'll be ready in a jiffy."

"Fried chicken!" Maggie exclaimed excitedly, throwing out some air punches for good measure.

"Oh, no, young lady," Rosie said as Maggie reached to lift the towel covering the chicken. "You go change and wash up first." Maggie picked her backpack up off the ground again and darted down the hallway to her room quicker than she could have said, 'Yes, ma'am,' if she had thought to do it.

Tammy bustled around the kitchen and smiled tiredly at Rosie. "What an afternoon," she announced.

"I'm sorry they all decided to ambush you like that." Rosie shook her head. "for a group of grown women, they sure know how to act like a bunch of children."

"Most of 'em mean well enough," Tammy sighed, "but I'm tired of people tellin' me what to do with my life. First my Mama, then Terry..." she trailed, off.

"Then Prissy?" Rosie finished for her.

Tammy nodded. She ran a hand through her honey-blonde hair. "Prissy's the most popular person I know. She was always good at everythin', in that way that a pudgy, uncoordinated girl like me could only dream of." She smiled wryly. "I thought myself lucky to be counted as one of her friends. Now I'm not so sure anymore. She doesn't seem to care how I feel about Terry. I think for her it's more about keepin' up appearances."

"I think you'd do better to keep your own counsel," Rosie advised her, "for sure."

Tammy nodded her agreement. "And I intend to."

Their grown-up conversation was interrupted by Maggie barreling back into the room, the smell of lavender hand soap still trailing after her.

Ka-chunk. Ka-chunk. Ka-chunk.

The steady rhythm of the dryer had lulled Rosie into a contemplative silence. It had been two days since Declan had left Fox Cottage. Having him there in the first place had felt so right, despite the minor inconveniences of having someone else in her home. Little things like gigantic boots kicked off by the door and hearing him snore in the living room seemed well balanced when she also had someone around who could do much-needed repairs on the cottage, and someone to have an adult conversation with. She hadn't even known him that long but she had a hard time keeping her mind from drifting to him or concentrating on what she was doing, and then that reminded her of everything else that had happened.

The door to the Kwik Kleen rattled open. A plump older woman wearing stained denim overalls bustled into the tiny laundromat, running a hand through her short white hair to straighten it.

"What a day!" she blustered, shoving the door closed behind her. "Wind'll blow the leaves clear off the trees long before they fall on their own!"

Rosie occupied the 'waiting area' of the Kwik Kleen, if you could call it that. She already occupied one half of the small outdoor-style bench seat beside the AC unit, and peered up at the other woman from beneath her bangs, her trashy out-of-date magazine forgotten. The woman noticed her, and then did a double take.

"You're Rosie Bell," she declared, holding out a hand. "Maude Merriwether."

Rosie shook Maude's hand, noticing that her skin was rough like tree bark and that her nails were cropped savagely short. "Guess my reputation precedes me," Rosie said, offering Maude a wry smile.

"Priscilla Bishop's *mouth* precedes you," Maude corrected her, bustling forward with a laundry bag. She stuffed sheets and towels into the vacant machine. "Not all of us have the lack-of-sense required to listen to 'er. Pleasure to meet ya!"

Rosie's smile grew in both width and feeling. "I'll keep that in mind." She wished that Maude's reputation had preceded *her*, because she was completely at a loss as to who this woman was. And she was dying to know why Maude seemed to have beef with Prissy.

Maude added her detergent, closed the machine's door, and fed her spare change in. When she hit the 'start' button and the machine obliged her by starting immediately, Rosie stared in disbelief.

"Wait—how did you do that?" Rosie asked, awestruck.

Maude wedged herself onto the rickety bench between Rosie and the questionable window AC unit. "Do what?"

"Make the machine just... work like that."

Maude seemed confused. "You just press the button and it turns on," she said slowly, as though Rosie was a special kind of idiot. She huffed.

"Just like a fella, really. All's ya gotta know is which buttons to push, to have him rarin' to go. Gentlemen, start your engines!" She barked a laugh at her own joke, but her amusement was fleeting. She shook a finger in Rosie's direction by way of warning. "But your Irishman, now there's a different kettle of fish if I ever saw one. Crafty. *Real* crafty."

Rosie's ears pricked up and she looked at Maude with fresh eyes. It had been a whole forty-eight plus hours since she'd given him his marching orders, and while she was glad he seemed to have taken her seriously she would be lying to herself if she didn't admit that the whole thing had left a sour taste in her mouth.

"You know Declan?" she asked.

Maude huffed a light laugh. "Bless your heart," she said, rocking back in her chair and ignoring its squeak of protest. "I own the Beep'n Sleep out on the highway."

She leaned closer to Rosie and spoke under her breath as though she was worried about being overheard. "He arrived yesterday afternoon, lookin' for a room. I didn't like the look of 'im, so I put him in Number 15. Right next to my office!"

She sat up straight, nodded once as though

to say 'you're welcome', and then added gruffly: "I'll keep a close eye on 'im for ya. And the Dames don't take too kindly to anyone who's up to no good! All the men in this town have gone plum crazy, no two ways about it."

Rosie didn't know whether to laugh at the thought of Declan being monitored by Maude or to wince because even Maude knew that they had been 'a thing' and now that thing was over. Her heart had just decided on the latter, tears stinging the back of her eyes in a way that made her balk with horror just as her dryers beeped in tandem.

"That's me," she murmured with relief, stepping over to retrieve her laundry. She normally would have folded it before putting it back in her laundry bag, but she didn't want to hang around and hear any more gossip about her recently-estranged-housemate-slash-potential-boyfriend. She stuffed her clothes in, knowing she would regret the wrinkles by the time she got back to Fox Cottage.

"Thanks Maude," she said, reaching for the door handle. "See ya 'round."

"Hope so," Maude replied blithely, picking up the magazine that Rosie had abandoned. "Real conversations are rare as hen's teeth in this town."

The irony that none of her conversations with Declan had been 'real' either bugged Rosie all the way to collect Maggie from school.

TAMMY'S CAR, A SIMPLE BUT CUTE SEDAN WAS PARKED on the lawn near the house when Rosie and Maggie came sauntering up the drive. The walk was quite pleasant now that the overbearing presence of summer had dissipated; the scattering of leaves that played in the breeze and the sharp tang of pine needles in the air made Rosie excited that Fall was creeping into town.

Maggie ran ahead, leaping up the porch steps like a miniature mountain goat. She was through the door before Rosie could call out to her to be careful, and the tell-tale sound of voices that drifted towards her as she climbed the porch herself told her that Maggie was already regaling Tammy with tales of her day.

Rosie locked the screen door and then closed the wooden door behind her to ward off the sneaky evening chill. The smell of pumpkin spice hung in the air, and her stomach did a backflip in anticipation. There was definitely pie in the kitchen. Having Tammy in the house was both delightful for her palette and disastrous for her waistline.

"Hey girl," she smiled as she entered the kitchen, just in time to see Tammy hand a potato peeler to Maggie. "What's cookin'?"

"A feast fit for three queens," Tammy announced,

nodding her head in the direction of the small oven in the corner. Rosie could see a roast chicken crisping up inside. A pumpkin pie was cooling on the cooktop.

"Glad we don't have four-of-a-kind," Rosie teased, washing her hands. "It smells so good that I'd hate to have to share it!"

Tammy fixed Rosie with a proud smile, and Rosie grabbed a bowl of peas that needed shelling. "How was your day?" she asked Rosie lightly.

"Not bad," Rosie replied. "I met Maude Merriwether at the Kwik Kleen."

"Oh!" Tammy exclaimed, and it was clear from her tone that there was more she would like to say on that subject, once there was no chance of them being overheard by a small person. Rosie glanced at her friend with a smirk, her eyebrow hitched in amusement. They both looked at Maggie, who was only halfway done peeling her first potato, her tongue poking out of the corner of her mouth as a measure of her extreme concentration.

"Well," Tammy said slowly, clearly trying to work out a way around the situation but still get her point across. "Maude's an absolute pillar of the community. The Beep'n Sleep is the only place in town you can get work done on your car, and there's nowhere else for people to..." she trailed off, as the implication of her next word hit her a little too late. "Stay," she finished awkwardly.

As though on cue, Maggie's ears pricked up. "Isn't Declan coming home for dinner? You only said three Queens, Tammy. What about our King?"

Rosie fought back a cough and paused, pea in hand, to look at her daughter. "Well, that's why it was so strange I should bump into Maude, honey. Declan has decided that he needs a bit more space than we have here, so he's gone to stay with her at the Beep'n Sleep."

Maggie lowered her potato, looking crestfallen. "Why?" she asked, "doesn't he like us anymore?"

"It's not that, Pumpkin," Rosie assured her. "It's just that the couch is really small, and there were four of us here trying to squeeze into a tiny cottage." She leaned toward Maggie and pressed a kiss to the top of her head. "This way you get your own space back, and Tammy can sleep on the couch for a while."

Tammy nodded subtly from her side of the kitchen and held up a 'perfect' sign to compliment Rosie's save.

"I guess that makes sense," Maggie said quietly, focusing on her potato. "I sure will miss not having him here, though."

"I won't miss his snoring," Tammy teased. "It sounded like an elephant was in the living room!" Maggie giggled in response, and the mood in the kitchen lifted a little.

Rosie picked up the pace with her peas. When all the vegetables were peeled, Maggie excused herself to shower.

"Damn" Rosie sighed, throwing down her pea. "What a day." She could feel her sadness and disappointment rising, but she was determined not to let it get the best of her.

Tammy took one look at Rosie's face and then threw down the dishcloth she had been holding, completing the circle. For a second Rosie thought she had offended her by cussing, but when Tammy reached into the tiny pantry and retrieved a bottle of wine Rosie was so relieved she could have kissed her.

"Open this," Tammy instructed her, shoving the bottle in her direction, "and tell me all about it while I finish dinner."

"I don't believe it!" Tammy gasped much later, when they had eaten a fabulous dinner and Rosie had spoken with Maggie and smoothed things over.

"Believe it!" Rosie told her. After having given her friend the non-magical explanation about what all Declan had done—even since before her arrival in Mosswood—Tammy's eyes were as wide as saucers.

"And after everything your ex-husband put you through. Shame on him!"

"Yep!" Rosie agreed heartily, crawling across the

living room carpet towards the coffee table. She poured them both another glass of red wine, and then took hold of hers and pointed in Tammy's direction with it. "That's the thing about men," she said slowly, her words a little slurred. "You think you can trust them—they *make* you trust 'em— and then *whoosh!*" She made a jerking motion with her free hand. "They pull the rug right out from under ya!"

"I know exactly what you mean," Tammy sighed, reclining on the couch that had become her new bed. "Terry's just the same. And any time I had the nerve to complain, he'd just go on and on about how lucky I was!"

"He was the lucky one! You should never have looked twice at Terry Holt. Man was punchin' above his weight for years!" Rosie let out a huge burp that made her blink in surprise. "'Scuse me!" she said, and then laughed at the shocked expression on Tammy's face. But her mirth was short-lived.

"The other thing that really grinds my gears," she announced, "was the way he—Declan," she added, "just expected me to fall for him? Like he didn't think he had to work for it at all, not even a little bit?"

Tammy blushed, looking sheepish. "To be fair, though, he *is* the Irish equivalent of a Greek god. Do the Irish even have gods?"

Rosie swallowed a mouthful of wine. "Beats me! I'm just mad at myself for falling for his act. I mean, he wasn't perfect and neither am I. But I called him out for being a dick more times than I can count and I thought he was... well..."

"*Improving!*" both women said at once, which cause them to burst into laughter. But Rosie's amusement and courage-in-commiseration soon turned to scorn. Her smile melted away, revealing a scowl that leeched the warmth out of the bonding session.

"I hate that I nearly slept with him," she admitted. "My experiences with men—well, with *Randy*—didn't lead me to feeling like I was worth much, by the end. Declan pretended to be so much more than that, and then *wasn't*. I can't believe how quickly I fell back into that trap!" She swiped a tear from her cheek with the back of her hand, lifting her head to smile weakly at Tammy. "Seems like I oughta know better."

"Why should you?" Tammy asked, sounding surprised. "God teaches us all about forgiveness, as Prissy keeps tryin' to remind me."

Rosie snorted in a very unladylike fashion, but Tammy continued. "I don't think even the Almighty would judge you for not being able to forgive your ex-husband. But there's nothin' wrong with forgivin' men in *general*. There's plenty more apples in the barrel, and not all of them are rotten. You're not to blame for being brave and giving Declan a chance, hon. No more than I'm to blame for hopin' all these years that Terry was still faithful to me when my instincts told me otherwise. Whether we choose to forgive *them* or not is one thing—but forgivin' *ourselves*..." Tammy quieted a little, then continued sagely, "That's what's important."

This pearl of pure wisdom was completely unexpected, and surprisingly profound. Rosie stared at her friend and then, having no other response to offer, simply lifted her glass into the air and nearly sloshed some over the side. "I'll drink to *that!*"

And then she did.

# CHAPTER SEVEN

"P izza?!" Maggie shrieked, abandoning the jigsaw puzzle Rosie had borrowed from the Public Library for them earlier that day. She galloped around the room on an invisible horse. "Yeehaw!"

"Naughty cowgirls get *zero* pizza," Rosie said calmly, picking up to dial the number for Minetti's as Maggie stopped in her tracks. The phone rang out and nobody answered. "They must be busy," she sighed. Well, shit. She had just wanted to order her kid's favorite dinner so that they could enjoy a little luxury, for goodness' sake.

"Oh, there's no point calling them until at least eight," Tammy added, putting a puzzle piece in its correct location. "They're always busy for dinner, and takeout service is a whole other ballpark."

Maggie's face fell, and Rosie felt terrible for not having called through to the restaurant before mentioning the 'p' word. The whole exercise had been dreamed up as a way to spend some fun, quality time with her daughter and now it looked like she was going to have to scramble to come up with a backup plan.

"We could just drive down and order at the counter?" Tammy suggested. "We'd get served quicker that way, and they have a fish tank in the restaurant that I bet we would all enjoy watchin' while we waited!"

Maggie lit up again, and Rosie worried for a second that she would fizz and pop altogether like an over stressed lightbulb.

"Are you sure?" she asked Tammy, stressing the words so that her friend would realize what she was potentially signing up for: an hour in a restaurant waiting area with a kid who lived for her next pizza fix.

"Why not?" Tammy beamed, "It'll be fun!"

Bless her sweet, innocent heart.

Maggie turned to Rosie, her face frozen in an expression of hopeful exuberance. "Can we, Mom?"

Rosie smiled, and Maggie let out a whoop of excitement.

Minetti's wasn't just 'busy'; the place was packed like a tin of sardines. Rosie had never seen so many people happy to be crammed into such a tiny space in all her life. Patrons quite literally sat shoulder-to-shoulder, and it was obvious that there were some people sharing tables that didn't know each other at all.

The cacophony of voices, clattering dishes, and good-natured shouts from the kitchen rushed up to greet them as they slipped through the door and approached the counter. A young woman behind the counter smiled at them as they approached.

"Well hi there, Mrs. Holt!"

To her credit, Tammy didn't flinch. She slipped back into her role as Southern Homemaker as though she hadn't just recently walked out on it.

"Hello yourself, Natalia," she smiled. "How's the family?"

The girl rolled her eyes good-naturedly. "Same old." She paused. "Sorry to say, if you're after a table, we haven't got any free."

"We'd just like to order some pizza," Rosie called, leaning across the counter slightly so that she could both hear *and* be heard. "Takeout."

"Sure!" Natalia reached for a well-used pencil that was tucked behind her ear, held it above a notebook that was on the counter and then glanced back at Rosie. "What can I get you?"

But Rosie's focus had shifted entirely. Instead of being on ordering, she was staring at a table in the far-right corner of the restaurant that was small enough to offer a modicum of privacy. No strangers sat at either end of it, and the view over the romantic Chickasaw River outside looked magical. But more interesting than the table were the people sitting at it.

One of them was the rude, statuesque blonde woman who had peered through the window of the Go-Go Mart. This evening she didn't look like she was posing for a safari photoshoot with Vogue. She looked drop-dead gorgeous in a sleek plum-colored dress that folded elegantly over itself in draped pleats at the neckline; modest, but alluring. Her blonde hair was swept up in a style reminiscent of Ava Gardner's curls, and her teeth were supernaturally white beneath her velvety-looking dark lipstick.

The other person at the table, with his back to her, was Declan.

In the exact moment that Rosie noticed them, the woman noticed *her*. Glacial hazel eyes narrowed with malicious glee, and the woman's smile suddenly seemed predatory. She reached out a manicured hand, stroking Declan's arm. Rosie couldn't remember the last time she'd had a professional manicure, but she would bet her whole left hand that she had *never* in her life had one that expensive.

And then the woman's reflection in the window next to their table shifted without *her* shifting. It moved, turning in to face the restaurant, and Rosie could see that it wasn't her reflection at all. Skin fell in long shreds from the face of the creature she saw, stringy hair showing in a horror-movie version of the one the woman at the table was wearing. Rosie gasped.

"—Ma'am?" Natalia asked her, wearing a slight frown beneath her baseball cap and looking at Rosie as though she might be having some kind of episode. Tammy's hand came to rest on her shoulder, snapping her completely back to the Land of the Lucid.

"Oh—I'm sorry!" Rosie said, blinking and forcing a small smile. "Mental blank!"

Natalia seemed reassured. "No problem," she smiled. "I know what you mean. What would you like?"

Tammy's gaze had followed Rosie's across the room, and came to Rosie's rescue. "I'll have a pepperoni, with peppers and onion—and extra of everything."

"Mom," Maggie said, sidling closer to her mom and wrapping a small arm around Rosie's waist. "Who's that lady sitting with Declan?" she asked quietly, showing a surprising amount of restraint for her age.

Rosie swallowed. "I'm not sure, Pumpkin," Rosie added. "Probably just one of his friends."

Maggie pulled a face, cuddling closer to Rosie. "She looks mean."

Rosie looked down sharply at the top of Maggie's head, which was all she could see from that angle. It was probably a good thing her daughter couldn't see the 'wtf' look on her features. The woman, whoever she was, looked perfectly normal... at the moment. But what if Maggie had seen what she had just seen?

"What pizza would you like, Maggie?"

Maggie snapped back to attention, not unlike the way her mother had done moments before. "Bacon and cheese, please," she trilled, before untangling herself from Rosie and going to almost press her nose again the glass of the fish tank closer to the door."

"And for you?" Natalia smiled in her direction.

She wasn't hungry anymore. She felt sick in her stomach, like she'd been sucker-punched. "I'll share with Maggie—thanks," she added as pleasantly as she could, pressing a hand to her abdomen. She gratefully allowed Tammy to pay for the meal, and the pair of them sat down together to wait.

"I'm sorry you had to see that," Tammy said in a low voice. Her expression was the same sweet, pleasant one she usually wore but her tone was overflowing with concern. "Are you alright?"

"I'm fine," Rosie lied, dragging her hand away from rubbing her tummy. She crossed her arms so that she wouldn't be tempted to go over to that table and strangle Declan into oblivion. Then again, she could probably work her magic on him right where she sat. That would teach the fucker to—

"The pizza will be a while," Tammy surmised, not sounding convinced. "Want me to drop you and Maggie back off at home? I can come back to—"

"And go to all that trouble?" Rosie shook her head, determined. "Not a chance. Thanks Tammy." She offered her friend the most genuine smile she could muster, and then set in to watching Maggie enjoy the fish.

Rosie didn't eat any pizza, and she certainly wasn't in the mood for leftover pumpkin pie. By the time Tammy went to bed it was clear that she was well on her way to being very worried, despite Rosie's assurances that everything was perfectly fine. Rosie puttered around the cottage for a while, picking up the accumulated household mess of the last few days.

If only it was that easy to clean up the mess in her relationships.

When she was certain that both Tammy and Maggie were fast asleep, Rosie slipped out of the front door and locked it behind her. She could hear the call of Mother Moon, and she couldn't refuse to answer. The sensation had built steadily over the weeks since she had first performed her ill-fated attempt at hearth magic. At first it had only been a vague inclination, kind of like saying to herself that she wouldn't mind a stroll around the garden in the moonlight.

But soon the garden hadn't been big enough to contain her. Rosie had ventured farther and farther into the woods with each weekly expedition, wearing less and less clothing to do so. Tonight she was only wearing a spaghetti strapped tank top and a tiny pair of cotton shorts, and her skin broke out into goosebumps as she stepped across the porch.

But as soon as she entered the pool of milky moonlight that fell across the garden, the chill in the night air melted away like she was slipping into a warm bath. The protectiveness of the moonlight even worked against such things as the weather, and Rosie smiled serenely as she made her way to the now-familiar path she had made for herself through the scrubby young pine trees and into the heart of Needlepoint Woods.

Animals scurried this way and that in the darkness. Rosie had mostly become accustomed to their comings and goings, and for the most part she was happy to ignore anything that sounded raccoon-sized or smaller. She passed beneath a tree that had half-fallen, brushing aside a thick curtain of Spanish moss as she went. Her feet were bare, but the leaves underfoot weren't yet old enough to have become crunchy. Instead, her toes sunk into the damp, rich soil greedily, craving the connection.

And then she felt a strange pang.

She stopped in her tracks, inhaling sharply and holding it as she waited to see if the sensation would strike again. It did, and it hit like a viper this time— hard, and fast. A stabbing pain flooded the front of Rosie's head and she moaned with pain, doubling over as the feeling first arrived with startling power and then went just as quickly as it had come.

"What the fuck..." she murmured, pressing both hands to her temples. She waited several moments for a third attack but when none came, she decided to investigate. Having anything nearby that could illicit that kind of a response needed to be dealt with, and soon. If there was danger in her woods, then she needed to be nipping it in the damn bud.

Her long chocolate brown hair was free of its usual ponytail prison, and it alternated between flowing majestically behind her like a true Witch Queen and flapping irritatingly in her face like one of those face-eating aliens from that one sci-fi movie when the wind suddenly changed direction. She turned her head this way and that, feeling out for the odd hum of energy that had accompanied the attacks but fearful that she might find the pain instead.

After walking for what seemed like an eternity Rosie wandered through the underbrush and out into a small clearing. Suddenly, it was as though Mother Moon forwent her promise of protection. Her skin prickled with goosebumps once again, and she didn't like the malicious way the breeze whispered among the tops of the pine trees. The only thing in the clearing was a thin rock, standing upright on its own in the center of the space.

There was no grass. It looked as though it had burned away to ash, leaving behind only dirt that felt gritty and hostile beneath Rosie's feet. No flowers, even though this part of the woods usually held beautiful blooms. No stray trees. And then the realization of what Rosie was seeing hit her, and she was chilled almost to her very core. There was no life in this clearing.

Only death. And it was very, very hungry.

She gulped down another breath, almost sobbing,

and regretted it immediately. The air tasted sour on her tongue, tainted with the blood of many animals that had seen the strange rock in this clearing and never lived to tell of it. Rosie turned and sprinted forward, crashing through the woods back the way she had come. She was determined that she wouldn't be joining them, but that strange stone in the middle of the clearing had looked like some kind of altar.

An altar that was craving her blood.

# CHAPTER EIGHT

Rosie had been looking forward to Friday all week. Tammy was off to run errands all day and had offered to drive Maggie in to school, and it was her day off work. And what that really meant was that as soon as she had packed out Maggie's sack lunch, made sure she was ready to roll for the day, and seen both of them off—she could get right back into bed again. Which was exactly what she'd done.

After discovering the black altar in the woods, the sensation that something big and bad was coming had only grown stronger. Rosie had made sure to strengthen the protection wards around the cottage, determined to provide what protection she could for Maggie, Tammy, and herself. She had briefly considered destroying the altar altogether, except she was worried it would cause whoever had built it to come forward. If only she was on speaking terms with Declan. She could have used some magical advice.

Her tiny bedroom at the front of the cottage hadn't been much when they'd moved in, but a woman's boudoir was her sanctuary, or so they said. Always on the look-out for creative ways to get ahead, Rosie had found a shelf where the ladies at Wood & Wax kept their mis-tinted paint on sale. Her bedroom was a beautiful dusky rose color as a result, and combined with the frilly white duvet cover she had picked up for $5 at the thrift store together with some string lights. A few plants were dotted around the room courtesy of Needlepoint Woods, planted in cheap terracotta pots she'd found in her garden shed out back.

She snuggled under the covers with relish, planning to hide from the world for a little while. Her dreams the night before had been troubled, plagued by what she had seen and felt in that strange clearing. She had kept getting flashes of a nasty smirk framed with dark lipstick, and a wide-brimmed hat that tilted up so the wearer could look at her but instead of being the beautiful woman Declan had been with, the face of the person was blank like a mannequin, but in flesh.

It was easier to brush these invasive nightmares away during the light of day, and before long Rosie had fallen back into a blissfully dreamless sleep. She might even have stayed that way, if it hadn't been for a tell-tale noise out front on the lawn. A noise that, Rosie thought as she pried her eyelids open with an enormous amount of sheer will, sounded exactly like a lawnmower.

Oh no.

She threw back her soft, heavenly blankets and leapt over to the widow. Creeping to the side, she pulled the curtains aside just enough so that she could survey the front yard with one bleary eye.

Declan was walking methodically across the front lawn, guiding her battered old manual mower in front of him. She watched him for a full three seconds, arms extended and triceps flexed as he went, and then she realized that he must have broken into her garden shed to get the mower out because the bastard didn't have his keys anymore. As though he knew he was being watched, he glanced up toward the house.

Rosie panicked, leaping back from the curtains with a barely restrained yelp. In her haste she kicked her pinkie toe on the corner of her bedside table.

"Fucking-fucketty-shit-shit-*ass!*" she grunted through gritted teeth, trying to stay as quiet as possible. Hopefully if she could keep everything on the down-low, she could pretend like she wasn't home. The last thing she wanted right now was an awkward confrontation with Declan, and that seemed to be the very thing he was after by rocking up to her house unannounced to cut her grass.

She flopped onto the bed on her back, lifting her knee to her chest so that she could gingerly massage her throbbing toe. She laid there for a bit, waiting for the pain to subside, and because he was fresh in her mind and she could still hear him pushing the mower along, her thoughts predictably turned to Declan.

Would he really come and mow her lawn if he didn't care about her? She'd made it pretty obvious the other day that they were no longer romantically linked... hadn't she? Yet here he was... being helpful. It wasn't that she couldn't mow her own damn lawn, but it sure was nice having someone else to do it for her. Even better when that someone was 6 feet and four inches of pure muscle with an accent to die for.

That realization sat with her for a few more seconds until she decided that so long as he was happy to wander around on her lawn half naked, she might as well look. She got out of bed again, albeit this time it wasn't as enthusiastically as before. She re-assumed the position at the window and pushed aside a sliver of the curtains.

And Declan was sitting on the porch swing just to the left of the porch steps, playing with his phone while the lawnmower pushed itself around the yard. Blood rushed up into Rosie's brain, threatening to spew out of her ears like a volcanic eruption. He had come over to mow her lawn to try and crawl back into her good graces, and when he had thought he'd given it enough time to check if she was home or not, he'd opted to use his magic to finish the rest of the job!

Un-fucking-believable.

Gathering herself and not caring a bit that she was still wearing pajamas that were printed all over with tiny teacups, Rosie marched for the door. She unlocked it and wrenched it open loudly in a way that made Declan jump and then pushed through the screen door.

"What do you think you're doing?" She put her hands on her hips and glared at him. All of the frustration and upset from the past few days culminated in her expression, and the effect wasn't lost on Declan. He balked but managed a smooth recovery.

"Mowin' the lawn," he replied candidly, waving a hand at the mower to further highlight the obvious. "It was overdue—I'd planned to do it last week."

"It's my lawn," Rosie told him through gritted teeth, "and that there is my mower!"

He looked at her calmly. "I know that, love. I just thought you could use a hand is all."

"I am quite capable of mowing my own lawn," she hissed, "especially if all you can be bothered to do is use magic! I wouldn't have even *needed* the mower, if I intended to use magic to do it!"

His nonchalance glitched and she saw a flash of awe cross his face. "Really? You've been practicing hedge magic too, then?"

"What I do," Rosie said coolly, drawing herself to her full height as she stared down at him from the porch, "is none of your damn business. And neither is my lawn."

Declan grinned. "Spoken like a true Queen."

She didn't flinch. "Spoken like a true asshole. I told

you to leave here and let me and my kid get on with our lives."

"For Christ's sake it's just lawn, Rosie!" He threw his hands up in the air, his bravado in tatters. "I just wanted to do something nice for you. I haven't seen you in almost a week."

"And what a lovely week it's been! It reminds me of what life was like before you decided to start dictating my circumstances." Rosie planted her hands on her hips defiantly. "Magic isn't the solution for everything, Declan. Some things need to be done the old-fashioned way."

He opened his mouth to respond, but then closed it again when he couldn't think of anything to say. He was saved by his own truck rattling up her drive and skidded to a halt on the gravel in front of her lawn. Rosie's eyes narrowed to slits when she saw blonde bangs peeking out from beneath the headscarf worn by the driver.

Declan looked up to note her arrival and groaned, forcing himself out of his comfy position on the swing. Rosie stopped on the top porch step, her shoulder pressed reassuringly to one of the support posts. When Declan didn't immediately start moving in the direction of the car, the woman tooted her horn.

"Better go see what your girlfriend wants," Rosie told him venomously. Declan threw Rosie a helpless look that only served to piss her off, before he walked across the lawn towards the truck. The woman turned off her engine, as though she wanted Rosie to be able to hear.

"I thought you said you wouldn't be long?" The woman complained with a pout as Declan approached. "If I had known that you were going to be mowing lawns for lonely women, I wouldn't have made our appointment."

"I'm not finished here," he said, glancing back towards Rosie.

"Oh I think you are." With a negligent wave of her hand, the woman sent the mower over onto its side with a dull clunk. She smiled brightly, and Rosie felt her blood, which was already boiling, reach atomizing point. "Come on," the woman clicked her fingers at Declan several times. "We're going to be late."

So he had told this woman that he would be here, but not why he had come. By Rosie's way of thinking, men only told a woman where they were going if that woman had a vested interest in their goings on. And what appointment could they possibly have together? A week ago he had been ready to serve her grapes on a silver platter, talking about how they could fulfil the ancient prophecy of their people. Now he was climbing into his truck with another woman, glancing at Rosie over his shoulder and hesitantly waving to her.

She flipped him the bird.

The truck kicked up dust as it peeled away back down the drive, leaving Rosie's vision even more clouded than before. If Declan was that quick to run into the arms of another woman, was anything they had actually real?

It was a good thing that Ben didn't mind Tammy tagging along with Rosie to her shifts, because the motherly woman had become something of a fixture at the Go-Go Mart. There was only so much cleaning that could be done, however, and once all the shelves were fully stocked there wasn't much else to do besides serve customers.

Saturdays would have been a likely candidate for the busiest day of the week for the Mart, but the weekend farmer's market nabbed most of the local business. Country folk were more inclined to buy farmer-direct, and did the majority of their crockery shopping on Saturdays and Sundays. Perched on the banks of the river downtown, the market occupied the large parking lot next to Mosswood Bakery and was conveniently located near both The Moon Cafe (which served amazing flavored coffee) and the local playground.

Rosie loved going to the market herself, and she and Maggie had visited several times. Unfortunately it meant that Saturday or Sunday shifts at the Mart were always going to be slower than a wet week. Tammy flipped through the latest issue of *Southern Living*, chatting occasionally about this and that. Rosie checked her phone again, noticed that there were no new messages, and then slid it back in her pocket.

It had become something of a habit for her, and she didn't know how to feel about it. On the one hand she was relieved that Declan hadn't texted her. On the other, her days were strangely lackluster without a small tiny ping here and there to announce his latest missive. If it wasn't for the fact that she liked to have her phone to hand in case the school needed to call her about Maggie, she might have turned it off altogether.

She sighed, and both her and Tammy looked up just in time for somebody enter the store. Or rather, two somebodies. As if the day wasn't already trying enough, God chose that moment to unleash Prissy Bishop on them both. And right there, joined at the elbow with her, was Declan's new woman. They both wore turtlenecks and matching smirks.

"Why Tammy," Prissy purred as the pair waltzed up to the counter, "I reckoned we might find you here, seein' as you're no longer baking at Church on Saturday afternoons." She ignored Rosie completely, which is more than could be said for her companion. The other woman only had eyes for Rosie, and it was an interest that Rosie was happy to return.

She glared at the women, color rising to her cheeks as her blood pressure kicked itself up a notch. Just who the hell did they think they were? Rosie hitched up her brow and her metaphorical big-girl panties, and refused to back down. The stare-a-thon continued until Prissy became the unintentional referee.

"This is the lost soul I was tellin' you about," she whispered loudly to her companion, obviously angling to be overheard.

Tammy looked from Prissy to the woman and back again, starting to realize that this wasn't just about Prissy checking in on her out of the goodness of her preachy little heart.

Tammy replied politely, with as much of a smile as she could muster, "I don't mean to be rude, but I'm not actually a lost soul." She glared in Prissy's direction, and Prissy blinked as though she couldn't believe her eyes. "You see—" Tammy continued, but she was cut short before she could get started.

"—I mean," Prissy laughed breathlessly, glancing at her friend playfully and flashing her a quick roll of her eyes before she delivered the main insult, "if up and leavin' your husband don't mean you're a lost soul, then I don't know what does!"

Tammy's expression was flatter than a roadkill raccoon. "I left my *cheating* husband, after giving him every chance in the world over the years to *not* be unfaithful to me. And I've had just about all of this conversation as I can take, Priscilla Bishop."

Prissy's mouth fell open and for once she seemed at a loss for words, but her friend—Declan's girlfriend— came to her rescue.

"Prissy only mentions it because I'm a marriage counsellor. I'm in town this week to deliver a guest sermon at the Church tomorrow on forgiveness in matrimony, and Prissy thought you might benefit from my Ministry."

It was Tammy's turn to be stuck for a response. She was obviously surprised to hear that the irritatingly elegant woman was part of the Church too; a Church that she hadn't had anything to do with for the past few weeks now. It had been a huge adjustment for her, and where she would have once been a member of 'Mosswood's official welcome wagon', being on the outs with her religion was beginning to take its toll on her.

"Well," she replied eventually, her voice thick with forced politeness, "it's a pleasure to meet you, Miss..?"

"*Mrs.*," the woman corrected Tammy with a saccharine smile. "Mrs. Gemma Forrest."

"As in Forrest Gump?" Tammy asked sweetly, but Rosie was still too frozen to appreciate Tammy's hopeful quip.

"No, as in *Declan* Forrest. I'm his wife."

And now she really did know the truth. Gemma wasn't just Declan's old flame, or even a current one. She wasn't just some woman he had picked up because he had balls black from her turtle-ex-husband and blue from her not being ready to take that leap yet. She was his fucking *wife*, as in *present*. He had been living with her for months, sleeping on her couch, making out with her, doing handy things around the house so that she could both admire his practical skills and his abs at the same time.

Randy might not be the only human-turned-reptile in town, when she got her hands on Declan *Forrest*.

"Well," Prissy continued, practically gloating, "we hope that you'll think about coming down for the Sunday Service tomorrow, don't we Gemma? I'm sure everyone would be happy to see your bright face back amongst the flock. And who knows?" She turned to Rosie, and even though her smile was cemented in place her eyes were devoid of any warmth. "You might just learn a thing or two."

"Thank you for thinking of me," Tammy replied, seemingly before she could help herself. The two women took their time seeing themselves out, but as soon as the door had closed behind them, Rosie let out an aggravated huff. She sank downwards, her resolve melting until she was draped across the counter with her head turned towards the CCTV screen so that she could watch the two women on the camera outside, getting elegantly into elegant Gemma's stupidly elegant convertible. And then she saw it again.

Lines filtered downwards from the top of the screen, so quickly that if she had happened to blink then she would have missed what happened next. As Gemma got into the driver's side of the car, the footage seemed to glitch and for a full second, Rosie saw her for what she really was. A hunched, wrinkled old hag with a long, drooping nose and skin that hung off her bones. And then the vision was gone. Rosie blinked a couple of times, decided that she *had* just seen that, and that she really needed to talk to Declan—for more reasons than that he had a fucking wife this whole time and decided not to tell her.

"There's no fucking way on God's green earth I am ever setting foot in that Church," she declared. "Not tomorrow, not ever."

"*Language*," Tammy reminded her, aghast.

Going down to the Beep'n Sleep after dinner probably wasn't her best plan of attack, but when Tammy offered to stay with Maggie *and* lend Rosie her car it was too tempting to pass up. She wasn't going to sleep that night anyway, thanks to the million-and-one thoughts buzzing noisily around her head. She might as well tell Declan what she thought of him—and his freaky-looking wife—and get it over and done with.

Twice now Rosie had seen the strange shift in Gemma's appearance. On the first occasion, Rosie had thought it might have been a trick of light and shadow playing on the glass of the restaurant window while the river shifted outside. But seeing it today in black and white on the CCTV camera, even for just a second, had convinced her that this wasn't something she could just push to one side. There was something very, very wrong with that woman.

Rosie pulled into the parking lot of the Beep'n Sleep and immediately spotted Declan's rusty old truck parked next to what had to be Maude Merriwether's tiny black Smart car. She smiled ruefully as she pulled up alongside both. She liked people who were true to their word, and it looked like Maude really was keeping an eye on Declan. If Rosie had cared about what Declan may or may not have been getting up to, she might have offered to buy the old woman a cup of coffee and a doughnut at Granny's just to get the goss.

There were fifteen rooms, all in one line stretching from the back of the property to the office. The lights outside of each room were automatic, so the area was well lit. Rosie could make out a large workshop across the parking lot, but it was locked up securely for the night. All in all it seemed a neatly run little business, and Rosie approved. That was until she saw the chicken.

It was perched on the railing that ran between the porch supports, yellow eyes almost orange in the manufactured lights from the fluorescent globes above. It cocked its head to one side as Rosie approached, regarding her with an avid curiosity that actually made her feel a little nervous. If she was going to be accosted by free-range hens *and* wives, Rosie might just call the whole damn thing off.

She skirted the chicken's immediate vicinity. Its head lifted and then fell in a little bob, and it offered Rosie a small noise by way of greeting. "Hi there, hen," she said to it, slowly moving past and towards the motel door that had a small sign saying '15' on the wall beside it, and a pair of Declan's boots kicked off haphazardly by the door. One of the tongues lolled out of boot like a happy dog, and Rosie could clearly see a brown speckled egg sitting inside. "That's no place for you to lay your eggs now," she clucked disapprovingly. "Shouldn't you be up in your roost for the night? It's gettin' kinda late to be out." The chicken didn't respond, so Rosie decided to mind her own business.

Knocking on the door was bound to be the hardest part. She hadn't seen Declan since Lawngate, and she was still furious with him for that—and a bunch of other reasons. They were stacking up, one of top of another, and she knew it was only a matter of time before it all came crashing down around her. She wasn't looking to rekindle anything they might have almost shared; she wanted to warn him about what she had seen, tell him what she thought of him, and mosey on home.

She knocked, and the sound of footsteps followed. The security chain was being jiggled in its track, and then the door opened to reveal Gemma, wet hair swept up into some kind of fancy hair turban and a standard-issue white motel towel wrapped tightly around her willow form. Water still glistened on her decolletage. To say that Rosie was taken aback was an understatement, but she supposed she shouldn't have been. It was perfectly acceptable for him to be living with his wife. She bitterly wondered where he had been planning on *her* sleeping, if Rosie hadn't kicked him out of Fox Cottage.

Gemma wore that same infuriating smirk carved into her lips, and she popped a hip so that she could rest a manicured hand there. "Yes?"

Rosie felt even more unsure of herself now than she had on the drive over. She steeled herself, forcing her spine straighter and her voice to be clear and not wobbly. "I'd like to speak to Declan, please."

"Sorry. He's..." With a glance over her shoulder as though to check something, Gemma looked back at Rosie. "*Indisposed.*"

Oh. *Oh.*

"Oh," Rosie said out loud. She was the world's biggest idiot. She was a moron for having let him get close to her in the first place, and she was stupid for letting him move into her cottage and into her and Maggie's life. And she was an absolute imbecile for rocking up to his place after dark to warn him about his actual wife like some pathetic love-sick stalker. She had nothing else to say, which was just as well because the door had been closed in her face.

She stumbled past the hen, startling it into a short-lived flight from the porch railing and down into the parking lot itself but she didn't care. She just needed to get out of there. Tammy's car started without a fuss and Rosie kept hold of her self-control long enough to drive slowly out of the lot and turn up the road leading up to the cottage. As soon as she passed the abandoned Hayes Sugar and Syrup mill, she pulled over onto the side of the road and turned off the engine.

"Fucking asshole jerk-off sonofa*bitch*!" she screamed, hitting her hands on the steering wheel so hard that she thought the airbag might deploy.

And that's when she started to ugly cry. Not because of Declan's manipulation, or his duplicitousness, or because Gemma seemed to be determined to torment her. Rosie let her tears fall in long rivers down her face and neck, and she rested her head on the wheel because she was too exhausted to do hold it up any longer.

She wasn't crying because she had lost something she hadn't realized she'd wanted with Declan. She was crying because she'd never had anything real with him to begin with.

# CHAPTER NINE

"I can't believe you talked us into this," Rosie hissed at Tammy, who was sitting on the pew to the left of her, with Maggie on her other side. The room was rapidly filling up with people that Rosie hadn't even known existed in Mosswood and the surrounding area—and a few that she wished didn't. Prissy was standing to one side of the dais talking to the Pastor and Gemma, who didn't look like she cared a bit whether Tammy and Rosie were in the room. Terry sat nearby, scrubbed up in what Rosie assumed were his only 'good' clothes. Every so often, he shot sad-eyed looks over at Tammy in a way that made Rosie want to roll her eyes. He was talking to a man in a Sheriff's uniform that Rosie assumed to be his brother.

"Don't look now," Tammy warned her in a low voice that she obviously didn't want Maggie to overhear, "but Declan just arrived."

"Fuck," Rosie muttered under her breath. An elderly woman with tight brown curls cropped close to her head turned to tut and glare, and then glance at Maggie who was reading the church program and swinging her legs happily.

With a sigh, Rosie sat back and at least tried to appear like a good God-fearing Christian. And in many respects, she *was*. She tried to be a good person, and do right by others. She just didn't think she needed four walls and a roof once a week to prove that she had a relationship with the Almighty. Although maybe they weren't as square as she thought, given that her life had been nothing short of an emotional roller coaster since arriving in Mosswood.

The thought of using marriage-counselling-via-sermon to fix her toxic relationship with Randy was enough to make her laugh-out-loud, and she might have if she didn't catch a glimpse of an impossibly large person trying to squeeze themselves into the pew behind her out of the corner of her eye. He was going to sit right behind her and marvel at the way his wife preached to a congregation of people she considered way beneath her?

*Fan-fucking-tastic.*

Rosie blinked and stared ahead, determined to ignore Declan even if it meant pretending to pay attention to the service. Pastor Myles had taken his place behind the pulpit, and a respectful hush had fallen over the congregation.

"Good morning," he said, in a way that seemed more formal than his greeting at her cottage not so long ago.

"Good morning," echoed the audience unevenly, including Tammy. Whoops, thought Rosie. Missed that cue.

"Let's take a moment to welcome each other to His house." Everyone smiled, looked around, and made an effort to greet those around them. A few people even turned to say good morning to Tammy and Rosie, which made her feel as though she were suddenly in the spotlight. More than one pair of eyes had stared her way when they had walked in, but now the feeling intensified. Rosie looked up just in time to see Myles grin in Tammy's direction. Tammy blushed, offered him a tiny, self-conscious wave, and then looked down at her Bible.

Rosie quirked a brow which tumbled straight into a frown when a familiar voice whispered behind her.

"Rosie, we need t'talk."

He had leaned forward to help his voice carry, and she could feel the warmth of his breath on the back of her neck. It made her feel gross and she tilted her head away from the airy contact in a move reminiscent of the hen the night before. A man sitting in the row in front of Rosie shifted in his seat uncomfortably, and Rosie focused her efforts on ignoring Declan while Pastor Myles introduced Gemma.

"Look" Declan whispered, "you have every right to be angry with me. But I just want to tell you that—"

"Shh!" The elderly woman had turned in her seat and was fixing Declan with such a ferocious stare that Rosie felt shamed by osmosis. She could feel her cheeks starting to redden with embarrassment, and she moved down her pew a little closer to Tammy in the hope that some of her Christianity would rub off, because right now she felt like committing a first-degree felony in the house of the Lord.

Fortunately, she was saved from the possibility of twenty-five to life by Gemma taking her place behind the pulpit. The woman smiled generously at the room. Rosie suddenly wasn't sure that this would be the salvation she'd been hoping for.

"Hello, everyone, and thank you, Pastor Bishop for that stellar introduction." She paused and took a breath. Her gaze had drifted across the room and when it fell to where Tammy, Declan, and Rosie were sitting, interest sparked in her eyes.

"My name is Gemma, and I'm here today to talk about forgiveness. Now you might think that forgiveness comes easy to us. Here we are, God's children, doing the best we can to live in His grace. We give our hearts and souls in prayer, show charity to those who need it, and are good to our neighbors."

Rosie didn't mean to do it. She hadn't planned it. But a snort escaped her before she knew what was happening, and it echoed into the rafters of the church like a bird taking flight. She tried to cover it with a cough as Pastor Myles straightened his tie.

Gemma continued. "But the true measure of a good Christian is being able to let go of the things that hurt us so that we can move forward into His light."

Several people in the audience were nodding, including the elderly woman sitting in front of Rosie.

"After all," Gemma continued, "Doesn't God forgive us for *our* sins? Doesn't He say 'ask and thou shalt receive'? When we, in our darkest and most tumultuous times go to God and ask him for absolution, does he spurn us and cast us down?"

"No!" someone near the front of the Church said passionately. Gemma nodded at them, her smile having settled into an upwards curl of self-satisfaction.

"Of *course* He doesn't," she agreed. "And why? Because Our Heavenly Father trusts that we will learn from our mistakes, and grow, and become better people for it."

Rosie glanced at Tammy out of the corner of her eyes, curious to see how her friend was doing in this very conveniently timed guest sermon. Tammy was staring straight ahead, listening attentively with her hands in her lap in a very ladylike fashion. Worry licked the inside of Rosie's stomach like the beginnings of a fire that could easily turn wild. She hoped that her friend wasn't going to have her head turned by a few pretty words and a seemingly repentant husband.

"What we can learn from this," Gemma was saying,

"is that when we are asked for forgiveness by those who have wronged and hurt us, it is our Christian duty to accept them back into our hearts. Harboring animosity is a sin, and it's also bad for your health." The congregation was peppered with polite laughter. Gemma smiled again, looked around and then leaned towards the microphone. "Please turn your Bible to…"

Rosie had stopped listening. She hated that Gemma's sermon had a logical point, and one that ninety-nine percent of the people in this room would swallow hook, line, and sinker. Hopefully Tammy wouldn't be one of them, though Rosie didn't like her chances much. She knew how important the Church was to her friend, and she couldn't blame Tammy for wanting to remain part of the biggest community in town. After all, she knew from personal experience how difficult life could be when you were on the outs with Prissy Bishop—Rosie was just lucky enough that she didn't care.

Her mind turned to thinking about Declan. She could feel the low-key buzz of his energy behind her, reaching out towards her like one pole of a magnet seeking its opposite. It was a small but stark reminder of the good times they had spent together during their short acquaintance, and it pained her heart. She'd had good times with Randy, too, in the beginning. She might have been a little more inclined to be generous with her forgiveness and hear Declan's side of the story, if she didn't think that it would become a slippery slope to putting up with a whole lot more of that behavior down the road. And she knew what putting up with something you shouldn't led to.

⊱————

The air outside the Church was sweeter than she'd ever smelled in her life, save for the air the night she had bustled Maggie into a cab and left Atlanta for good. Rosie stood on the stoop, looking down the rolling green hill into Lee Park. The tops of the huge trees there swayed in the light breeze. She could see clear down to the river from here, and she watched the bubbling water rushing through the bend that would take it along the waterfront, past the farmer's market.

Maggie ran around on the grass with a few of the other kids. Tammy had gone to thank Prissy, the Pastor, and Gemma for their ministry. All the other folk were milling around out front, soaking up the last of the late summer sunshine. Rosie watched Tammy blush and smile her way through saying goodbye to Pastor Myles before she was cautiously approached by a few other people who obviously wanted to say hi. Rosie smiled, watching Tammy releasing herself back into society like a wounded deer who'd needed a little time to find her feet again.

Rosie's gaze trailed inevitably over to Gemma, who

was holding court among a gang of enthusiastic parishioners. Declan was nowhere to be seen, which didn't seem to bother her any. She was happily laughing with Carol-Ann Wallace from Wallace Realty, Sheriff Holt, and a young woman Rosie didn't recognize. As she passed through the crowd, networking, people gravitated towards her and she seemed to leave a string of impressed-looking people in her wake. Rosie felt actual bile rising into her throat.

A moment later, Tammy materialized out of the throng of people who were leaving the building. Rosie took one look at her friend's face, and raised a brow.

"Well?" she asked. "What did you think?"

"I think," Tammy replied with a forced smile, "that I'm ready to get out of here. Let's go."

Rosie nodded agreeably, hands on her hips. "How about a walk through the park?"

"Awesome!" Maggie grinned.

# CHAPTER TEN

**M**onday morning was always a blur of getting dressed, having buttered toast, and the hasty brushing of teeth. Rosie had only just finished rinsing her mouth when she heard a knock at the door. Tammy went to answer, and Rosie made another mad dash to her side when she heard her friend gasp, "What are you *doing* here?"

She skidded to a halt next to Tammy, who was standing with the screen door still closed gaping at Terry on the other side of it. He was wearing dirty hunting clothes and had some kind of camouflage painted across his face. It was clear that he was either on his way to or from the woods, and Rosie raised both eyebrows when he produced a bunch of gas-station flowers from behind his back.

On the way *to* hunt then... and obviously not just deer.

"I thought you'd like these," he said holding them out to Tammy. She still didn't open the screen door, and Rosie was proud enough of her friend's resolve that she took a few steps backwards down the hall to give them a little privacy.

"After yesterday's sermon at Church, I figured I owed you an apology," he continued on. "I haven't been a good husband, and I know that now. But there's blame on both sides! If you just come on home, we can work this out without needin' to involve others."

Tammy was very quiet. Her hair was covering the side of her face in such a way that Rosie couldn't tell if she was smiling or crying, but neither would be ideal in this situation. When she finally spoke, her voice was a deathly whisper. "I will never go anywhere with you ever again."

*You go girl!*

"You're bein' bull-headed about this!" Terry exploded, and Rosie heard the sound of the cheap bouquet hitting the deck. "You've had your head filled with nonsense, and you're not thinkin' straight. All you have to your name is your car. The house, our savings, my retirement—everything else is in my name. Without me, you're not worth nothin' to no-one!"

"Not yet, maybe," Tammy agreed placidly. "But I expect that'll change once we've been to court. From what you'll have to pay me in alimony alone, I don't know that you'll be able to afford to scratch your behind, much less all the beer and cigarettes and cable TV you've been accustomed to."

Maggie had come down the hall to stand at Rosie's side, and she turned to usher her back to the kitchen as Terry really got going on the porch.

"You hoity-toity bitch!" he yelled, kicking the screen door. He then started on a string of vitriol that Tammy ignored as she shut the front door in his face and then locked it tight.

Maggie's eyes were wide as saucers as Tammy came to join them in the kitchen. "I'm sorry y'all had to witness that," she said, closing her eyes. "His bark's worse than his bite."

"Don't apologize for him," Rosie said, setting up a fresh pot of coffee. There was little point calling the Sheriff—he was Terry's younger brother after all. Coffee and a real breakfast seemed the order of the day. Maggie would just have to be late to school. And if Terry Holt didn't leave her property immediately, then the newer and much stronger protection wards that Rosie had set up around the cottage after the Randy incident would see to it that he was sorry.

After ensuring that Terry had gone on his way and multiple assurances from Tammy that she was 'perfectly fine', Rosie borrowed her car to drop Maggie at school. Her shift wasn't until that afternoon, which meant that she had time to take care of a little personal business before then. Terry's half-assed apology—brought on by Gemma's ridiculous sermon and the insistence of Prissy Bishop to stick her pointed nose where it didn't belong —had made Rosie decide to have it out with Declan once and for all. Whether for better or worse, she needed to get everything off her chest.

Tammy was right; forgiving yourself was important. And she needed to forgive herself for believing in someone who hadn't deserved it. She couldn't have known that he was manipulating her. She couldn't have known that he was already married when he had decided to pursue a 'prophesied relationship' with her. But she *did* know that her powers were growing stronger with each day. She experimented with plants, and nature, and the elements around her regularly, and her control was becoming steadier. And now she needed to stabilize herself so that she could move forward.

The Beep'n Sleep looked like a very different place in the light of day. The siding of the buildings looked like it had once been a bright and cheerful red, but it had now faded to a patchy rust color and the parking lot was in pretty bad condition. Chicken droppings seemed to decorate all of the walkways and railings. The door of the mechanical workshop was open and one car was parked inside. Rosie could see how cluttered it was and was surprised. Maude had seemed like such a sensible, well-controlled person.

She ignored the dust in the windows of the currently empty office as she parked up on the visitor's side of the office, cutting the engine and getting out of the car as quietly as possible. She didn't want to risk facing off against Gemma again—she'd rather sneak off back to the car if Declan wasn't about.

As she approached the door of Room 15, she could hear angry voices inside. It sounded like Declan and Gemma were having a disagreement, and Rosie's ears instantly pricked up. She crept closer, thankfully unhindered by feathered watch-birds, and listened as hard as she could.

"You're being unreasonable about this," Gemma sighed, her crisp English accent smoothing the irritation out of the edge of her voice. "Our families have been friends for centuries. We share ancestors. I'm not from some long-lost bloodline, trying to claw my way back into society!"

Declan barked a laugh. "You can have a bloody pedigree chart drawn up for all I care." There was a sound, like someone large throwing themselves into an armchair. "Rosie and I— our lines are promised to one another. A binding, magical contract. It's not the sort've thing ya can just let go."

"What about the promise you made to *me*? 'Til death do us part, for fuck's sake!"

"Ugh!" Declan's tone was long-suffering. It was

clear that this wasn't the first time they'd had this discussion. "We both know that wasn't even real, Gem. Stop pretending as though we were both in it for the long haul."

It was Gemma's turn to laugh. It sounded glassy; smooth, and completely transparent. "You were the one who asked me to marry you!" she shrilled, "not the other way 'round, remember? My family were less than impressed. I had a lot of fast talking to do."

"My memory's better'n yours," Declan snarked. "The only reason we even did it was to piss everyone off, and you know it. Or have you conveniently forgotten that detail?"

"No," she hissed. "I haven't forgotten that you wanted to marry an Englishwoman to spite *your father* who wanted to send you on a mission to find your poor, lost little Queen—wherever she was." There was silence for a moment. "Tell me," Gemma purred then, her voice taking on a gleefully spiteful note, "would you have been turned off if she'd still been a grubby gutter-rat in a string of broken homes when you'd found her, instead of some beautifully-fractured woman only a decent haircut and a good wardrobe away from looking the part?"

"You're skating on *very* thin ice, Gemma. Watch yourself."

She laughed again. "I don't need to watch myself. I'm watching *you.* Falling all over yourself for some washed-up biker mole and her brat."

A loud bang sounded from within the room that made Rosie jump, following by the sound of rattling glass. She realized Declan must have hit his fist on a table. "That's enough!"

"You don't *get* it, do you?" she wheedled, trying a different tact when disbelief, emotional blackmail, and straight insults had already failed her. "If you take her home, you and your entire kingdom will be a laughingstock. No one in the Circles really *expects* you to be joined with some—"

"Well then won't they get a surprise," he interrupted her. He sounded like he was white-hot with anger. Rosie could hear it boiling in his throat, ready to melt anything in its path down the ashes. "Because I'm either goin' home *with* Rosie, or I'm not goin' home at all."

"You care about the prophecy," Gemma said, sounding smug. "I get it. But look—you don't even *need* Rosie to fulfil it. It took me a while, but I've worked it all out." When she spoke next, Rosie could hear a sleek smile in her tone. "All we need is Rosie's *blood.*"

"You leave Rosie's blood where it's at," Declan warned her ferociously, "Or you'll need to be worrying about your own."

Rosie had heard enough. Her head was reeling from the flood of new information she'd just been swept away by. She needed to regroup and clear her head. Stumbling away from the door, she made her way over the to the car without even a hint of the care she'd taken getting out of it. Within moments she was speeding away towards downtown Mosswood, leaving the Beep'n Sleep and her growing doubts about Declan behind.

The dark, fresh water of the Chickasaw river hurried along, carrying fallen leaves with it as it made its way steadily south-east through town. Rosie used to think dark water looked dangerous, like it was full of secrets and bad vibes, but she felt very differently about this water. It was comforting, somehow, like a whole universe waiting to be explored beneath the first foot of clear water.

She'd seen the lookout from a distance many times but had never had an excuse to check it out in person until now. A tidy path led from the main waterfront shops right along the river's edge, and was popular for cyclists, joggers, and children on scooters. The lookout sprang up halfway along the riverfront and was little more than a large rotunda that was set into the water. A railing went all the way around, encouraging people to lean on it to better commune with the river. Rosie was only too happy to oblige.

To say that she was shocked would have been a massive understatement. She didn't know what she was more ecstatic about, that Declan wanted to be with *her* and not his wife, or that he had never really felt that way about Gemma to begin with. It was an interesting reaction, and on digging deeper she realized that while she might not be able to trust him not to overplay his hand, she *could* trust him with the most important thing in her life.

Maggie.

When he had been dying on her lawn during the altercation with Randy and his bikers, Declan's first thought had been for Maggie's safety. For all his faults, Rosie knew that if she showed him how his actions would affect her or Maggie, he would do better to *be* better. The revelation immediately lightened her load. Randy used to hurt—or threaten to hurt—her and Maggie in order to manipulate them both. But wasn't it the opposite with Declan? He had manipulated the circumstances around their new life in Mosswood, but he'd done it to take care of them, not keep them under his thumb.

On impulse she reached for her phone, unlocked the device, and dialed.

"Rosie?" Declan asked, surprised, as soon as he answered. "What's wrong? Are you okay?"

She closed her eyes as those words washed over her. They were the words of a man who actually cared. A stupid, misguided fool of a man, but a caring one nonetheless.

"I'm fine," she said, leaning over the railing so that

she could watch the river. "Are you busy? Can you talk?"

"Just gettin' ready for my delivery round. But I'll talk with you any time."

She took a breath to steady herself. "You said in Church yesterday that we needed to talk," she told him. "I'm listening."

"Thank you," he sighed, sounding relieved. "I just need you to know—yes, Gemma really *is* my wife. But it's not what you think," he rushed on to say. "That part might be easier explained in person. Point is, I don't love her. Never have, never will."

Rosie had already heard as much herself during her juicy eavesdropping session, but she reckoned she'd earned herself the right to make him sweat a little. "Oh?"

"I wasn't lying when I promised protection, faithfulness, and fealty," he said in a soft voice.

"Well, having a wife already is something of an obstacle."

"We're gettin' a divorce," he hurried to add. "It's why she's come. I got in contact with her, told her it was urgent. We got married in Vegas, so the paperwork has to be lodged in the US, too."

Rosie digested that for a minute. "You got married... in *Vegas*?"

"Not my finest hour," he admitted, "but I'd like to talk to you about it in person, if that's okay with you?"

"Not sure I wanna know," Rosie quipped dryly.

There was a short pause.

"So," they both said at the same time, and then laughed. Rosie hasn't realized it, but she had been cradling the phone so closely to her ear to absorb his voice that she was starting to get a crick in her neck. She swapped sides.

"So," he said again, taking the plunge. "Where to from here?"

"Dunno," she replied with blunt honesty, reaching up to tuck her hair behind her ears. "But I'm willing to try and trust you again on one condition."

"Name it," he said.

"That you never, *ever* use magic to interfere in mine or Maggie's lives again."

He didn't even hesitate. "You got it."

"I mean it, Declan," Rosie warned, wanting to impress the seriousness of the situation. "Swear it."

As she waited to hear his answer, Rosie began to gather her energy. She collected it from the part of her soul closest to her heart, holding it back until she heard his next words over the phone.

"I swear to you, Rosemary Bell," he promised faithfully, "that I will never use magic to interfere in your life again. I'm sorry. Truly."

She released the energy, and felt the familiar zing of her magic leaving her body. She held onto the railing in front of her.

"Thank you," she whispered, before having a sudden flashback to the night she had gone to his room at the Beep'n Sleep. "One more thing," she said. "I think you might have an egg—"

"Gah!" Declan yelped, and Rosie lifted the phone away from her ear to avoid the clatter of Declan dropping his on the ground. "Mother-clucker," she heard him growl in the background, accompanied by the sound of someone taking *off* a boot and peeling an egg-soaked sock off one foot. Rosie covered her mouth to stop herself from laughing out loud.

Declan picked up his phone. "You there?" he asked, agitation in his voice.

"Yes," she said sweetly. "Everything alright?"

"Peachy," he replied. "Aside from making scrambled eggs in my boot."

"That sounds unappetizing," Rosie quipped.

"You have no idea," he replied wryly. "I need to go talk to a woman about a chicken."

She smirked. "Good luck with that."

## CHAPTER ELEVEN

Late afternoon sunshine flooded the leafy riverside playground. A light breeze tickled the tops of the trees, sending playful shadows across the park. Rosie sat on a swing, thoroughly enjoying the breeze. Tammy occupied the swing beside her. Maggie played on the climbing frame in the sun.

"So," Tammy said. "How'd it go with Declan earlier?"

Rosie let the swing drift in time to the breeze, rocking back and forth slightly. "Better than I expected it to, if I'm being honest," she replied. "We still have a few things that need to be hashed out in person—including why he never told me he had a wife. But the major part of *that* is that they're getting a divorce. That's why she's here."

"Ooh," Tammy breathed, slowing her own swinging

down a bit so she could better look at Rosie. "So they're not—Y'know. Workin' things out?"

"Nope." Rosie sighed happily, letting the toes of her ankle boots scuff around in the dirt. "And he's promised not to—" she took out 'use his magic to be all up in my shit' and replaced it hastily with "—interfere in my business. Anymore."

Tammy nodded. "Well, I don't hold with prying, but I'm glad to hear y'all have mended your fences." She licked her ice cream. "You look good together. And he adores Maggie, plain as the nose on his face."

Rosie smirked, thinking about Declan's overlarge, crooked beak. "Sure couldn't get any plainer than that," she teased.

"Reckon Maggie's fond of him, too," she added.

"Reckon you're right," Rosie agreed, watching Maggie flip down from the climbing frame and canter towards the monkey bars.

"You've inspired me to do something a bit crazy," Tammy admitted, glancing sheepishly at Rosie. "I'm gonna ask Pastor Bishop if I can do a guest sermon this Sunday."

Rosie wasn't surprised that Tammy thought giving a sermon was a wild idea, but she *was* surprised that her shy friend was up for it in the first place. "What about?" she asked, genuinely interested.

"About standing up for yourself, and knowing your own heart," Tammy declared.

Rosie felt her chest swell with pride. By giving that

kind of sermon, Tammy would be all but tattooing a scarlet 'A' on her forehead, and it didn't seem like she cared a bit. "I think," Rosie told her, "that would be a brave and liberating thing to do."

"Will you come?" Tammy asked, sounding desperate. "If you and Maggie are there, I won't feel half so backwards in comin' forward!"

"We'll be there," Rosie promised without a hitch.

The afternoon settled like a mantle around the shoulders of the town, and for a while Rosie and Tammy sat contentedly, lost in their own thoughts. Maggie hung upside down by her knees, calling out to her Mom to watch her while she attempted all manner of dangerous maneuvers.

"Come on," Rosie said, "let's show this whippersnapper how it's done."

"How what's done?" Tammy asked, a tide of concern rising in her voice.

Rosie grabbed Tammy's hand and pulled her friend to her feet. "Can't be that long since you climbed a set of monkey bars," Rosie grinned, while Tammy attempted to literally dig her heels in.

"I don't think they're rated for—grown-ups," Tammy said, obviously referring to her weight.

Rosie shook her head. "They're steel bars cemented in the ground, Tammy," she prompted gently. "They're not *rated*, they're indestructible. How long have they been in this playground?"

Tammy knew when she was beaten, but she didn't like to admit it. "Since my mother's time, but—"

"No buts!" Rosie declared with a grin. "Come on. Live a little."

Those final words seemed to be the magic key needed to unlock Tammy's inhibitions. She didn't say anything, but she got to her feet and the two women trotted over to the monkey bars. Maggie, upside down with her long brown hair swinging beneath her, gave the pair of them a cheeky grin that would rival her mother's. Rosie smirked, and climbed up the ladder on one side of the bars while Tammy climbed the other.

"Are you gonna try and get up here, Mom?" Maggie asked, swaying from side to side so that she could feel her hair swish.

Rosie scoffed and threw a disbelieving look at Tammy, who giggled. "There's no try about it!" she declared, lifting a leg impossibly high. She swung it up through the first rung of the money bars.

Maggie let out a small but impressed "Whoa!"

Upside down and hanging by one knee, Rosie soon got her other leg through the gap too. And then she lifted herself up though the gap, pushing with her arms and wriggling her hips. For one horrible moment she thought she was going to get stuck. A horrific vision of having to be cut from the monkey bars by the local fire department flashed before her eyes, and she was just about to ask Tammy to give her ass a nudge when she managed to shimmy though.

Thank *goodness*.

Rosie popped up onto the top of the monkey bars, perching herself on top as though she was the queen of the castle. It was an interesting thought. She hadn't exactly had a lot of time to think about her future beyond putting the nastiness with Randy behind her. Then she'd been thrown head-first into helping Tammy, and then things with Declan had fallen apart in a rapid and spectacular fashion.

Gemma was still a concern, but Rosie had to wonder whether she was that much of a threat at all. Declan had declared his allegiance, and since their call earlier her heart had been a whole lot lighter. Maybe it was time to start thinking about what being a witch actually meant for her? Her monthly forays into the forest were a good start, but she really needed something more... something she could sink her teeth into.

The Queen bridge, she supposed, she would cross when she got to it.

"Cool!" Maggie declared, following Rosie's example and struggling until she was halfway through the gap in the rungs of the monkey bars. Rosie leaned over to help her the rest of the way up.

"There's no way I'm squishing myself up into one of them holes," Tammy announced, with a laugh. "But I can show y'all a different trick!"

"What trick?" Maggie asked with interest.

Tammy tapped the side of her nose slyly. "Just you watch," she said, amused. She swung along the rungs until she was further away from the start of the monkey bars, and then grunted and lifted herself up so that she was gripping the outside bar with both of her knees. Then she released both hands and began to swing herself back and forth. Rosie did feel a little concern; Tammy's jeans didn't look like they had great grip, and they were pretty high up from the sand below. She didn't like to say anything and ruin Tammy's trick, but her friend swung higher and higher until Rosie finally opened her mouth to say something.

But she was too late. Tammy had let fly from the bars, soaring through the air. She twisted mid-dive, and Rosie gasped loudly, preparing to jump down herself and go to the aid of her friend. But Tammy executed the twist and landed, stumbling a little on the landing but sticking it nonetheless. Rosie and Maggie gaped at her from the top of the bars, their mouths open in shock.

"Ta da!" Tammy sang breathlessly, fixing them both with a grin.

"Where'd you learn to *do* that?" Maggie asked, awestruck.

"I was a cheerleader," she laughed. "Junior varsity, before... well." Her grin tempered into a prim smile. "Before puberty hit."

"Cool!" Maggie beamed. "Can you teach me?"

"Only if your Momma says it's okay," Tammy said. Two pairs of eyes turned to Rosie.

It wasn't long before Maggie was hanging by both knees, Tammy standing in the sand beneath her and holding both of her hands. They were getting her used to swinging back and forth, while Rosie sat on top of the monkey bars watching with equal amounts of pride and dread. She felt a vibration in her pocket, and dug out her phone.

The lock screen told her it was a text from Declan.

A familiar flutter danced around in her belly, and a smile crept onto her face before she even realized it. She hadn't known how much she missed him. His little electronic notes always brought her a smile... but even more than that, they made her feel *special*. She didn't like to admit that she had come to depend on them to brighten her day, but there was no escaping it. Declan—reckless, goofy Declan—was someone she wanted to keep in her life.

She swiped through the lock screen and opened the text.

*Hope you're having a good day.*

Okay, that was pretty sweet. Things still weren't totally okay between them, and he had some explaining to do. But she was confident that, with time, patience, and honesty, they would be. She angled her phone for a selfie that would capture Tammy and Maggie beneath her, and the late afternoon sun catching the colors of the autumn leaves on the dark green grass. It was actually a beautiful shot, and she made up her mind right then and there to have it printed for a frame in the cottage.

*Chillin' by the river. Soul food.*

He started typing a reply straight away. Rosie

watched the three little dots bobbing up and down until it appeared.

*Great pic! Looks like fun.*

And then another.

*You look beautiful.*

Feeling heat bloom across her cheeks, Rosie typed back.

*Thank you.*

*You're welcome. I was wondering... it's been ages since I saw Maggie and Halloween is coming up. A while back I promised that I would take you guys to a pumpkin patch. Are you up for it later this week?*

*I'll let you know tomorrow*, she texted back.

The flutter in her belly became a full-on thrill. She knew that Maggie would absolutely love an outing to a pumpkin patch, but Rosie hadn't spoken about Declan to her since everything had gone south.

"Hey Mags," Rosie started, glancing at the time on her phone. It was starting to get around to the time they should be getting home. She started shuffling along the bars towards the end. "How would you feel about going to check out a pumpkin patch with Declan this weekend?"

"With *Declan*!?" Maggie asked excitedly.

Rosie grinned. Looked like she had her answer. "Okay, I'll let him know we can make it. You're welcome to join us, if you like Tammy."

"Oh," Tammy smiled, dusting off her hands. "I

think y'all need an outing on your own, but thanks for asking all the same."

"Thanks Tammy," Rosie smiled at her friend and then let herself down the side of the bars. When she was almost on the ground, Maggie made a flying leap to beat her.

"Ha!" The little monkey beamed, standing up with her chest puffed out. Then, straight out of left field: "Does this mean Declan's gonna be movin' back in with us?"

Rosie's heart skipped a beat. Why was it that her daughter seemed to be an expert at asking questions she didn't have answers for?

She wasn't about to make anything up, though. Instead, she shrugged. "I think it means we'll get to go to a pumpkin patch and do a bunch of really fun stuff," she said.

Maggie nodded, and then jumped with an "Argh!" She slapped a hand to her arm, looked at the spot she'd slapped, and then frowned.

"I just got bit by a mosquito,"

Rosie pressed her lips together. "Time to head on home."

ROSIE SAT ON HER BED, SOFT MUSIC PLAYING THROUGH her phone as she stared at the potted plants in the corner of her room as though expecting answers. By the time she had dropped Tammy's car off and stopped to have a sweet tea with her friend, she had already felt drained. After walking back into town, doing her shift, collecting Maggie from school and walking home again, Rosie was downright exhausted. She'd made basic Mac and cheese for dinner, and paired hers with a full-bodied red wine that was heaven to her lips. As soon as Maggie had gone to bed, Rosie had retired to her room with another glass.

Now that she knew where things stood with Declan, it was time for her to come up with a plan. It was clear that it wasn't going to be easy to get rid of Gemma. The woman had actually sounded deranged, what with all her talk about needing Rosie's blood to fulfil the prophecy. Just thinking about it now sent an eerie chill down Rosie's spine, and she took another gulp of her wine to ward off the bad juju.

She knew Gemma was playing a dangerous game. The hints of magic she had seen around the woman didn't feel like *regular* magic, or at least any that Rosie had encountered so far. It reminded her of the menacing altar in the woods, and Rosie was convinced that Gemma was behind creating that dark, dangerous place. Ugly was as ugly does, and for all her elegance, fine clothes and designer manicures, Gemma was ugly to her core.

But what was she going to do about it?

A little liquid inspiration couldn't go astray. Rosie padded out to the kitchen to refill her wine glass, noticing their old deck of cards lying in the middle of the kitchen table. They usually only used them to play Go Fish, but she wondered if they couldn't be used for much more than entertainment. What if she could use them in place of tarot cards? Her powers were developing steadily, and her intuition was getting sharper by the day. Maybe all she needed was a tool to help her find a solution to her own British invasion.

She went back to her room with the cards in hand, closing her door behind her. Tammy was watching tv in the living room. It sounded like a re-run of Days of Our Lives, and Rosie smiled and shook her head as she settled back on the bed, plopping the desk of cards on the blanket in front of her. She had absolutely no idea what she was doing, but she was desperate. If she could get any kind of insight that would give them the jump on Gemma, it was worth feeling a little silly for.

It didn't take long to find a webpage online for the tarot card meanings associated with playing cards. She briefly read a few of them, and when she was convinced that it was the right webpage to use for an impromptu fortune reading, she got down to business.

Shuffling the cards, she thought about their situation. The deck felt like it came alive in her hands, warming to her touch. Inhaling with excited anticipation, Rosie began to lay the cards out on the bed in front of her in a random-looking imitation of what she thought a tarot card spread should look like. First the Ace of spades. Then she turned over the two of spades. Then the three of spades. Nine cards in, Rosie glared at the perfect row of sequential spades before her.

"Very fucking funny," she muttered, swiping the cards back into a pile and reshuffling them. "Just tell me how we can get rid of this bitch. Be helpful, please!"

Rosie began to lay the cards out again, relieved when it looked like her request had been answered until a soft knock sounded on her door. She went to sweep them back into a pile before anyone could see what she was up to, but Tammy opened the door right away.

"Who are you talkin' t—" her eyes fell to the cards on the bed, widening with recognition and fear. "What in the good Lord's name are you *doing*?"

"Nothing!" Rosie lied, collecting the cards hastily. "Just playing Solitaire. I—"

"Don't lie to me!" Tammy glared at Rosie, and it was the first time she had witnessed her friend looking so angry. She imagined it must have been similar to the look she had given Terry, the other day when he had shown up uninvited with his weak-ass apology. Rosie felt ashamed of herself for lying, and she cast her eyes down before she looked back up again. Whatever else happened, Tammy deserved the truth. They'd been through too much together to give her anything less.

"I'm tryin' to get some answers about how to get rid of Gemma once and for all," she said, shrugging a shoulder. "I'm at a loss, and we just need her gone.

She's trouble, Tammy. And I don't think we've seen the half of it."

"Well I don't think Satanism is the answer, Rosie," Tammy whispered, as though even saying the name 'Satan' was a scary prospect. "You know better'n that. You even went to Church with me the other day!"

"I went to Church to support *you,* not because I had some deep-seated need to have Prissy glare at me for three hours uninterrupted," Rosie muttered back.

Tammy was silent. She looked from Rosie to the cards and then back again, as though trying to weigh the situation in her mind. "Well, I don't hold with occultism," she said eventually, and then sighed. "But I know that you've got a good heart. I know you think that what you're doing is right, and it's not for me to judge your actions."

Rosie relaxed a little. Knowing that Tammy wasn't going to completely flip was a relief. She'd come to Mosswood thinking that she didn't need anyone or anything except Maggie and a roof over their heads. But now that she had a friend in Tammy, Rosie knew that wasn't strictly true. She couldn't come straight out and tell her devoutly Baptist friend that she was a witch, much less potentially one of their queens. But having tested the water and not finding that it was freezing cold was a great comfort to her and gave her hope for the future. She smiled at Tammy, and Tammy smiled back and shook her head good-naturedly.

"Well, you came along to Church to support me,"

Tammy said, moving to sit on the bed beside Rosie. She folded her legs up under her, looking for all the world like a curious house cat. "How can I help?"

Rosie's smile blossomed into a grin. It was nice to think that they could see each other's differences, but still be there for each other when the chips were down. And with everything that had happened over the past few months, it was *glorious* to not feel like she had to handle everything on her own.

"I'm not really sure, if I'm honest," Rosie admitted. "I have this interpretation that I got off the internet," she waved her phone, "and the cards. The only thing it says we need is intent."

"Well our intent is to get that meddlin' piece-of-work outta our town and outta our *lives*," Tammy said forcefully. "So I'd say we got ourselves intent enough."

"Amen," Rosie agreed. She gathered the cards up for the third time, gave them a bit more of a shuffle and then held the desk out to Tammy. "Blow on it," she said.

Tammy looked at her like she had three heads. "You want me to what now? Why?"

"Dunno," Rosie admitted, "I just had a feeling that we should cover the cards with our intent, and that seemed the easiest way. Kinda like how you see those gamblers do on tv."

"Oh," said Tammy, seemingly happier with that answer than one that involved her giving her breath to Satan. "Well, alright then, since you put it that way."

She blew onto the deck in Rosie's outstretched hand, and then Rosie held the deck in front of her own face. She collected all of her feelings about Gemma, and then blew on the cards like she was making a wish on a birthday cake.

There was silence for a few seconds. Tammy looked around as though she was expecting a thunderbolt to rattle the house. "Now what?" she asked nervously.

"Now we find out if our wishes will come true," Rosie said. She began to lay out the cards, stopping when she got to three as the instructions on the website had said. Her hand felt weird and itchy, and she hesitated before flipping over a fourth card. Her hand still itched.

"How many do we need?" Tammy asked, watching with big eyes, the way a child might stare at their sibling getting a shot.

"I guess until I feel like we don't need any more?" Rosie replied. "I haven't done this before."

She laid out a fifth, then a sixth. By the time the palm of her hand had stopped itching, there were ten cards laid out in a row on the bed. Rosie reached for her phone.

"Okaaay," she drawled as she scrolled through the descriptions. "So. This card," she tapped the Queen of Spades as she scrolled down the website on her phone to read the description, "is..."

Rosie suddenly felt all the blood drain from her face. Goosebumps popped up on her arms and the back of her neck, and she suddenly realized that they might just be in for a whole dose of truth.

"Is what?" Tammy asked, her voice rising with panic. "What is it? Oh Lord, don't let it be anything bad!"

"It's Gemma," Rosie said, turning her phone around to show Tammy. "See? A ruthless and manipulative person. Gotta be!" She raised her eyebrow, even though she was feeling a little unnerved herself. "It's fine, okay? They're just cards. I'll take the Queen of Spades printed on cheap cardboard over the real Gemma any day of the week."

"I suppose you're right," Tammy agreed, glancing nervously at the cards. "What do the rest of them say?"

Rosie skimmed through the interpretations.

"This next one is a hot-headed risk taker—gee, I wonder who *that* could be," she added sarcastically with a roll of her eyes. She pointed to the King of Clubs. "This one is someone who is creative but forceful. And look! Between them is a two of spades, which means a failure to communicate or a misunderstanding of some kind."

"That must be you and Declan!" Tammy gasped, awestruck. "Holy crickets, this is crazy!"

"Yeah, so far it's pretty accurate. But it doesn't tell us how to get rid of her so far. Okay—this ten of Clubs is a big debt or responsibility. Placed between me and the Jack of Hearts, which is a gregarious, good-natured person. I bet that's Maggie!"

"Makes sense," agreed Tammy, smiling sadly. "Being a parent is a huge responsibility. You wear it well."

Rosie flashed her a quick smile. "Well shucks," she said, before the next description made her heart fill with love. "You're here too—look! The Queen of Diamonds." She read out the description. "A practical, warm-hearted, and dependable mother figure." Rosie reached over to squeeze her friend's hand. "Looks like we're in this together."

Tammy squeezed her hand right back. "Didn't need a pack of demon-cards to tell us that," she winked.

Their bonding moment was interrupted, however, when Rosie's attention skipped to the next card in the row. She frowned, and the goosebumps came back again with a vengeance.

"This is not good," she murmured, tucking her hair behind her ears before pointing. "This eight of Spades means powerlessness or feeling trapped, followed by a battle—the nine of Clubs. And then..." she trailed off, glancing first at the five of Hearts. It was the last card in the line-up, and it was the most telling of them all. She looked up at Tammy, fear clearly showing in her eyes.

"Loss," she whispered, "and despair."

The two women looked at each other, their eyes filled with fear.

# CHAPTER TWELVE

I t did Rosie's heart a whole lot of good to watch Tammy walk into church that Sunday morning with her head held high. There was no remnant of the shame or uncertainty that Prissy and the other church ladies had tried to instill in her. Instead, she was a confident and beautiful woman who knew her mind, and Rosie couldn't have been prouder. She and Maggie trailed behind toward the front of the church, ignoring the looks and whispers that were directed their way.

How sad that they were used to it.

They took a seat in the third pew back, leaving Tammy to go and greet Pastor Myles. He offered Rosie a smile, and gave Maggie a little wave which she forced herself to return half-heartedly. Church wasn't the most fun place for a kid with a whole backyard of woods to explore, she guessed. The rest of the flock settled into their places, chatting and laughing amongst themselves while they waited for the Sunday services to get underway.

While she was thrilled to be there to support Tammy, Rosie's mind had already fast-forwarded to later that week. They were heading out to Pineview Plantation on the outskirts of town with Declan, to check out their annual pumpkin patch and fall festival. Maggie was looking forward to choosing some pumpkins to carve for the porch, and Rosie could hardly wait to see what crafts were on display. But more than that, both Bell girls were looking forward to seeing Declan.

Pastor Myles took his place behind the pulpit in due time, beaming at those gathered before him. He greeted the congregation the way he had the Sunday Gemma preached, and again the congregation greeted him back.

"Welcome, everyone, to this humble house of worship on this bee-autiful Sunday morning! Our guest preacher this morning is a woman who will need no introduction to anyone here," he grinned, "but I'm gonna give her one anyway! She's a pillar of our community, both within Hand of God and beyond. The town just wouldn't be right without her in it!" He paused long enough to look across the front of the Church at Tammy, who was waiting off to the side. She was clutching a small stack of notes on index cards in front of her and looking nervous as hell, but Rosie watched her anxiety melt away under the warmth of the smile Pastor Myles shone in her direction.

"I'd like y'all to put your hands together and give a big ol' welcome to Tammy Holt," the Pastor finished, and the audience obliged—some more enthusiastically than others. The Pastor made his way to the side of the stage to look on, and Rosie couldn't help but glance around the room to take note of where his usually possessive wife was on this occasion. She caught sight of the tiny blonde woman clear on the other side of the Church and a few rows back from the front, glaring at her husband.

Prissy was shaking her head and trying to make it subtle, but her Farrah Fawcett styled curls shook violently with each attempt. A frown was desperately trying to crease her brow, but all she managed was a slight scowl. Looked like she'd earned that Botox after all.

Tammy was just taking her place behind the pulpit, and as much as Rosie wanted to be the attentive friend, she couldn't help but follow Prissy's gaze to see who she was trying to communicate with. Her husband was standing in his place, hands clasped in front of him and his easy smile as easy as ever. But Rosie noticed that his knuckles were white with the effort of gripping. She glanced back at Prissy, who was mouthing words Rosie couldn't make out from the side. Rosie's head ping-ponged back to the Pastor, who gave one determined shake of his head and tried to pass it off as shooing away a fly.

This was too good! Prissy clearly didn't want Tammy to be able to give her sermon today! Why not? She knew that Prissy only valued Tammy insofar as Tammy could do things for her or make her look more popular than she really was, but this was sinking to a whole new low even for her. Rosie's attention snapped back to Prissy to get her reaction to being told no, and caught the tail end of Prissy wordlessly arguing with her husband. And then Prissy glared right at her.

Whoops. Given that nothing could be done now that she had been straight up caught out, Rosie fixed Prissy with a smile that wouldn't have melted on a skillet full of hot butter. Prissy's face darkened like a pixie-sized thundercloud. Rosie grinned, and turned to look at Tammy as her friend cleared her throat.

"As Pastor Bishop said," she began, a nervous smile on her face, "Those of you who don't already know me from Church will know me from around town. I've been a Mosswood resident my whole life," she announced, sounding a little stronger, "and I felt compelled today to come and talk to you today about a subject that's been very close to my heart these past few weeks."

Tammy shuffled to the next note in her stack, read it and then looked up at the room. "Being betrayed by someone you love, care for deeply, and have put your whole heart into trusting is just about the most devastating thing that can happen to a person," she said. "I'm not saying this to dredge up my own personal circumstances," she added hastily with a glance at Prissy, "though I'm sure you are all intimately acquainted with them by now. I'm saying it because having that much hurt surrounding you is suffocating, and you feel as though you might never break free and breathe clean air ever again."

A couple of people in the audience nodded; Rosie was right there along with them. How many times had she felt that way because of Randy? More than she'd ever care to admit, that's for sure.

"At first you're scared to admit how hurt you really are," Tammy continued, "because you think that it somehow makes you weak, or because you'd rather live in ignorance and dress it up as bliss." She shook her head. "It isn't, and never will be. All that's doing is makin' the hurt fester. You put on Band-Aid after Band-Aid, hoping that one day it'll come away clean. But what happens when you run out of Band-Aids?"

Tammy reached out and took hold of a Band-Aid that she had put on the back of her hand, and slowly peeled it off. She'd drawn a big red dot on the back of her hand with a magic marker, and held it up to show everyone in the Church. "Hurt's still there," she told them with a helpless shrug. "It hasn't even healed a little bit. But that's where the Lord steps in." She took a cute checkered handkerchief out of her pocket and dipped the end into the glass of water that had been left for her on a table by the pulpit.

"You can pray on that hurt," she said, wiping the handkerchief over the dot. Some of the red faded, and she showed the audience. 'And that brings no small measure of comfort. But when you're talking about pain that cuts to the bone, there's still gonna be a little left when you're done. You can forgive the person who hurt you," she wiped the dot again, and a little more red came off. She held the remnants of the mark up. "But it still won't be gone. The pain's still gonna be there, lingering in the back of your mind.

"The only way," Tammy said, abandoning her notes and putting them on top of the pulpit so that she could step out to the side of it and address the congregation more directly, "to get rid of the rest of that pain, is something only *you* can know. Some find comfort in the passing of time, others in finding other things to occupy their minds." She wiped the dot again with her handkerchief, and the dot was finally gone. "But nobody ever fully cleansed their hearts of that kind of pain by being told *how* to.

"That's why it's so important to know who you are, and what you will and won't take," Tammy said. Passion was clear in her voice, and Rosie could see that she was feeling emboldened by the number of people in the audience who were nodding their heads along with what she was saying. "Knowing your own truth is a powerful thing and standing up for your own beliefs is nearly unbeatable. It doesn't mean that you're not gonna get hurt—we all do," she said, shaking her head softly as though to comfort anyone who might have been feeling how she herself had been feeling. "But when you step up and look that hurt right in the face, and tell it that you won't be beat—well." She grinned. "Then *it* will be beaten."

She stepped back behind the pulpit, and Rosie could tell that she felt like she was walking on air by the little spring in her step. She turned through her Bible to the reading she had marked. Rosie listened attentively through the story and meant to stay put for the rest of the service until she noticed Prissy slipping into the Church hallway out of the corner of her eye. The opportunity really was too ripe for the picking. Rosie passed by Tammy as her friend was returning from the dais.

"Be right back," she whispered, and Tammy nodded as she sat by Maggie.

"Thank you, Tammy, for that insightful sermon!" Pastor Myles was saying, his voice as jolly and upbeat as ever. "I'd like to follow it with a reading from..."

Rosie followed Prissy into the hallway, and then checked the ladies' room. No Prissy. The only other place she could be, then, was the kitchen as all the other rooms were off another hallway. She stepped into the kitchen where Prissy was doing some kind of measured breathing. She had her hands pressed to either side of her head, and her lips forced into an exaggerated pout.

"I don't mean to interrupt your little self-soothing session," Rosie said, making Prissy jump and wheel to face her. "But what the *hell* is your problem, lady? Tammy came down here to give a guest sermon at a Church *your husband* is the Pastor of! And you're trying to interfere with that?"

"You don't have a clue what you're talkin' about!" Prissy hissed, taking slow steps around the stainless-steel kitchen island. Rosie watched her with narrowed eyes and moved in the opposite direction.

"I think I know exactly how it is," Rosie said, not bothering to hold back her contempt. "You're jealous!"

"Me?" Prissy laughed scornfully. "Me? Jealous of *Tammy*? Really, now—have you seen her?"

"Oh, I know those words didn't just come out of your mouth Prissy Bishop!" Rosie growled. "Tammy is a kinder, more generous, more God-fearing woman than you'll *ever* be. You don't get to fat-shame her—not now, not *ever!*"

"Why don't you just mind your own coop, Rosie?" Prissy said primly, changing tact. "With so many hens all chasing the same rooster, I'd think you'd have enough on your plate without lookin' for more trouble besides."

Rosie felt her last fuck fly right out of her brain. She opened her mouth to give Prissy the serve of a lifetime, when Tammy appeared in the kitchen doorway. "There you are Rosie," she cooed, stepping into the room and sliding an arm through her friend's. "The service is done! Maggie's ready to hit the road," she grinned. The whole time she spoke, Tammy didn't so much as glance in Prissy's direction.

Rosie was impressed. Maybe Tammy had been paying more mind to how Prissy pulled everyone's strings than anyone had thought.

"Tammy!" Prissy yelped pathetically. "Are you coming along to the costume sale for the Harvest Ball? It wouldn't be the same without you!"

It was only then that Tammy gave Prissy her attention. She offered her the sweet smile that she was well known for, but for the first time ever Rosie noticed that it had a sharp edge to it.

"Why, I sure am," she said, sounding as though she was trying to hold back her excitement. "Pastor Myles has asked me to be in charge of it."

Prissy's mouth fell open, and it was everything Rosie could do not to laugh out loud. She had come in here to give Prissy a piece of her mind and find out why she was being so vindictive towards Tammy, but it really looked as though Tammy had everything covered herself.

With the parting shot delivered, Tammy grabbed Rosie's hand. "I'll need your help, of course, Rosie! Come on, we've got planning to do!"

The pair of them exited stage right, leaving a wounded and bitter Prissy in their wake.

# CHAPTER THIRTEEN

**N**ext Saturday, the crisp afternoon air was a welcome tonic as she wandered around the vibrant surroundings of the Pineview Plantation. The house itself was a grand affair, all white-washed glory with huge columns that gave its already stately appearance an air of distinction. The grounds were expansive and filled with fairground stalls, kiddy-rides, and the all-important pumpkin patch. A straw maze ambled off to one side, and the other was bordered by the thick expanse of the woods, which had started to dress up in their fall finery.

She didn't know if it was because she hadn't physically seen him for a while and apparently absence makes the heart grow fonder, but Declan looked *good*. His beard was neatly clipped into a masculine style that made him look more GQ than lumberjack, and his usual cargo-pants-and-flannel-shirt-combo had been traded in for a pair of well-fitted chinos and a slate blue knitted sweater that clung to his broad, muscled frame and set off his red hair.

His light, wooded aftershave had tempted her into breathing more deeply as they had driven out to Pineview Plantation. What was it about good, subtle aftershave that was so damned sexy on a man? They wandered together past a candy apple stall, and Rosie was just making a mental plan to double back and buy a few later when she caught another whiff of it. *Yum*.

"I'm so glad you were up for this," he said, strolling casually beside her with his hands in his pockets. "I've really missed you guys. It's really quiet at the Beep'n Sleep. That is, unless you count the bloody chickens."

She recalled the hen that had been outside of his door when she had come to confront him and found Gemma in his room instead. "And the estranged wife in your hotel room, wearing nothing but a bath-towel," she added bitterly before she could help herself.

Declan frowned and stopped walking to look at her. "Beg pardon?"

Rosie took a deep breath. "I came over to the Beep'n Sleep one day to speak with you, and she answered the door in a towel. Told me you were 'indisposed.'"

"What?!" Declan exclaimed, his voice loud enough to make several people nearby turn and look at the pair of them. Rosie felt her cheeks flush with embarrassment and hoped that she could pass it off as the chill in the air. She pulled her cozy cherry-colored longline cardigan closer around herself.

"Mom," Maggie interrupted, "Can we go through the maze?"

Rosie turned to look at Maggie, an unspoken rule in her eyes.

"Sorry," Maggie said hastily. "Excuse me, Mom—can we please go through the maze?"

"Sounds like fun," Rosie replied. "Why don't you go wait in the line to hold our spot, and we'll be right over."

Maggie skipped off happily, as Declan took a step towards her. She glanced up at him, always struck by how much taller than her he was.

"She has *never* stayed in my room," he told her earnestly. "She must have used magic to get into my room, because I doubt Maude would have given her a key. She's pretty by-the-book."

"She seems it," Rosie agreed, as they began to walk towards the line for the straw maze.

Declan hesitated for a moment. "Why did you come over?" he asked. "You'd seemed pretty determined to get me gone."

Rosie felt the same chill she'd felt upon seeing that strange clearing in the forest run over her skin now as she thought about it. She hadn't had a chance to tell Declan anything. "I want you to know that nothing that I'm about to say is being said out of jealousy," she told him, wrapping her arms around herself. "You need to know. I think Gemma's mixed up in some really bad stuff."

He frowned, watching her face. "What do you mean?" he asked. "I know she's not the sweetest pie on the cooling rack, but—"

"I found an altar in the woods," Rosie whisper-blurted, not really sure how else to say it. Declan's face went from concerned to 'totally done' in 0.02 seconds.

"Are ya serious?"

"One-hundred-percent," Rosie said. "It had this weird black rock, and nothing was growing around it. Nothing. Not even a blade of grass. And then there was this... feeling." She shuddered. "Like I could sense that there was nothing in that place except—"

"Death," he finished for her.

She looked at him sharply. "You've seen it?"

He nodded slowly. "Only once, and a very long time ago. We found a place like that—a dark altar—in the forest near my parents' court back in Ireland. Rosie," he reached for her hand, and even the warmth of his skin against hers wasn't enough to ward off the chill that the memory of that place brought her. "It's a place where blood magic is performed."

If even one tiny part of her was tempted to laugh at the ridiculousness of the words coming out of his mouth, the seriousness of his expression and the dread seeping into her own bones stifled it completely.

"There's more than that," she pressed on. "I saw

her that night you two were having dinner at Minetti's, and again when she came into the Go-Go Mart. Her face shifted and she looked..." She shook her head as she searched for the words. "Disgusting. Like her normal face wasn't there anymore, only this... *thing!* It was barely even human! It—" Declan squeezed her hand, bringing her out of her memories and back to the present. She looked at him, scared.

"...That doesn't sound good," he admitted.

"Ya think?" she asked sarcastically.

"Hey," he said, pulling her into a comforting hug. "Whatever she's up to, we'll deal with it. Together."

She let the feeling of his arms around her work its magic, calming her now that she had finally said what she'd been trying to tell him all along. She glanced at Maggie, who was almost to the front of the line for the maze, and reluctantly stepped back from the hug.

"I know," she said, meaning it. "You can tell me the rest of what you wanted to tell me in person once we're chasing my daughter through this maze."

He followed her over, but he didn't let go of her hand. As they stepped into the line, Maggie slipped a hand into each of their spare ones so that they formed a temporary circle. "Okay," she announced matter-of-factly. "Once we're inside, we're racing. Every girl for herself."

Declan raised a brow,

"You're an honorary girl for the day," Maggie added magnanimously, and he grinned back at her.

"That's mighty kind of you, ma'am."

"That's just the type of person I am," she replied, and she sounded so damn grown up that Rosie had to turn her head away to hide her smile.

As they neared the front of the line, they noticed a familiar face taking the tickets. Ben was dressed in full Civil War reenactment regalia, right down to the dirt smudges on his face. He grinned at the three of them as they approached and Maggie presented her ticket to him.

"Hi Ben," Rosie said, earning them all a nod in return. "I didn't realize that you were part of all this," she waved a hand at the event in general.

"Sure," Ben said, a little sheepishly. "I've been part of the local reenactment group ever since I was a kid. Used to do it with my Dad." He glanced up at the grand plantation house. "These days, I like to spend my time out here volunteering. Tours, events. That sort of thing. Helps me feel close to him."

Rossie nodded. "That's so lovely," she said kindly. "Be sure and let us know what your tour schedule is. We'd love to come along."

"I'll do that," Ben promised. "Are y'all headin' into the maze?"

"Yes!" Maggie exclaimed, jumping with excitement.

"Now don't go running off," Rosie warned her.

"Oh, you don't have anything to worry about around here," Ben assured her. "We've got soldiers stationed through the maze and at the exit," he winked at Maggie, "on the look-out for anyone tryin' to escape."

"Just the same," Rosie added, throwing a look at her daughter. "Stay close."

"Okay Mom!" Maggie beamed, taking off into the maze.

"We're never going to *find* her in here, much less beat her to the end," Declan muttered twenty minutes' worth of dead ends later.

Rosie smiled. "You heard Ben – she'll have to wait at the other end until we manage to make it through. In the meantime," she said, pausing as she glanced between a fork in the path, "we have enough privacy for you to fill me in on what all you wanted to tell me." She nodded at the left path. "This way."

He reached out for her hand, enveloping it in his as he trailed along dutifully behind her. She was worried but ready to hear everything he had to tell her about Gemma. Once they were both on the same page, they'd finally be able to move on from the situation.

"When I was younger, I wasn't always as... accepting of the prophecy my parents insisted I was duty-bound to fulfil," he admitted, sounding somewhat sheepish. "I was rebellious, and childish."

"Was?" Rosie asked lightly with a smirk, earning her a smirk back in return.

"My father, in particular, is very controlling and demanding. Because I'm his heir, he seems to think it makes me his property. I wanted to show him I'm my own boss." He shook his head, as though disappointed in the stupidity of his younger self.

"Gemma was one of those acts of rebellion. Our families have been allied for centuries, but my father always held them at arm's length. The English have long interfered in Irish affairs, whether it be witch business or mundane." He pressed his lips together. "The only thing I could do to prove to my Da' that I wouldn't be his pawn and marry some witch from a long-lost bloodline—no offence—was to marry someone else. And it kind of escalated from there to me marrying an English witch, which is tantamount to treason in my Da's eyes."

"And then you married her in *Vegas*," Rosie added, able to see the funny side. She'd married super young, thinking that she knew what she was about, too. She couldn't really judge him for having done the same.

"In a drive-through chapel," he chuckled. "Da' was furious when he found out, and insisted that we annul the marriage. But I wouldn't."

"Until now," Rosie mused. She stopped walking, turning to face him properly so that she could watch for his reaction. "What happened to make it so important all of a sudden?"

"I met you," he told her, drinking her in. "He sent me here, saying that the auguries had foretold of your being, insisting I come back to America and sniff you out with a powerful location spell. And then when I saw you..."

She was hanging on his every word. So, he'd been curious about a future he hadn't wanted. She couldn't blame him there. "And?" she asked, determined to have the rest of it.

"You were in the car," he said, his voice softer and quieter than Rosie had ever heard it. "You were sitting in that clunky old car belonging to your ex in the parking lot behind that feral bar he used to practically live at." His face was so sad as he remembered the moment. "I walked past, making for the back door of the bar. But really, I just wanted a closer look at this all-powerful witch who was supposed to be my fated Queen. I glanced through the window at you as I passed the car. And you were gripping the steering wheel so tightly that your knuckles were white, and you were crying. Maggie was right there, curled up under a blanket on the back seat. And you were..."

He trailed off, unable to finish his sentence. He swallowed, and Rosie felt her heart squeeze with a sudden rush of feeling for him. When his eyes rose to meet hers, he fixed her with a sad smile. "That was the moment, right then. I knew me Da' was right," his smile twisted, "much as I hated to admit it to myself." He tugged on her hand to slow her down, stopping them for a moment in their search for freedom from the hay-maze.

"You're the one, Rosie," he told her. She looked up at him through her lashes, tilting her chin towards the heavens as he began to lean in for a kiss.

"Am I?" she whispered back.

He held off from connecting just long enough flash her a grin and nod slightly. And then her world slipped sideways. She couldn't hear the general noises of the crowd, or smell the caramel popcorn or the pervading scent of the nearby pine forest. All she knew was him; his lips, his hand gently cupping her face, and the way that being this close to him made her feel both incredibly safe and like she was playing with fire all at once.

The kiss ended on a sweet note, with Declan managing to get one more quick peck in before Maggie appeared inexplicably in the maze behind them.

"Maggie!" Declan said, lifting his hand to the back of his neck. "How did ya get all the way back there?"

"It's my second pass through," she declared with a proud grin before she narrowed her eyes playfully at him and her Mom. 'I *knew* I would catch you guys smooching. Gross!"

"I *am* pretty gross, to be fair," he grinned down at her. "Sorry wee'an."

Maggie glanced at her Mom out of the corner of her eye, and then shrugged. "It's fine, I guess. Just maybe do it in private. Nobody needs to see *that*."

*Ohmygod,* Rosie thought to herself, her heart racing and her embarrassment levels totally through the roof. Being schooled by your pre-pubescent daughter about the appropriateness of public displays of affection was absolutely *mortifying*. And yet Declan just took it effortlessly in his stride, while she floundered for words to say that wouldn't make her seem completely called out or overly defensive. She was saved by the pair of them.

"Come on Mom! I'll show you guys the way out," Maggie announced, getting behind her and pushing against her butt. "Otherwise we'll never make it to the patch before all the good pumpkins are taken!" When Rosie let out a relieved chuckle, Maggie hurried Declan up in the same manner. At the first push he stumbled forward, acting as though he was no match for her super-strength. The idea was laughable—the dude was a *wall* of muscle— and Rosie laughed more freely.

"Steady on there, boss," he said to Maggie, who was grinning from ear to ear. "I'm a delicate flower, you know."

"Oh, we know," Rosie sassed him with a playful smirk, letting Maggie lead the way out of the maze.

Once Maggie hit the pumpkin patch, she became a

whirlwind of excitement and energy. Rosie might have thought it was unusual for a child to be that interested in a bunch of pumpkins, if it wasn't for the fact that the place was full of over-enthusiastic kids all looking for the perfect canvas for their Jack-o'-lanterns. Standing beside Declan and watching Maggie enjoying herself seemed like a perfect afternoon to her, and she sighed contentedly as she snuggled deeper into her cardigan.

"Hello, darling," a dry British voice intoned from behind her. Rosie turned to see that Gemma had all but joined them, standing a little to their right. "I wondered where you'd got off to. I suppose I should have known," she smirked.

Rosie was biting her tongue, and Declan bit back a sigh. "What do you want, Gemma?" he asked, sounding bored.

"Well, isn't it obvious?" Gemma asked innocently. "I want my husband back." Declan barked a laugh, and Gemma glared at them both.

Maggie chose that moment to run up, eyes alight. "Mom, I found the perfect one! Quick, we need to get it before someone else does!" She then looked up at Gemma, hesitation creeping onto her exuberant little face. She stepped backwards twice, wedging herself between Rosie and Declan. Rosie reached instinctively for her daughter's hand. Declan slipped a strong arm behind the both of them.

"Well, hello there," Gemma purred at Maggie, leaning forward in that way that people have when they want a better look at a cute kid, but Rosie wasn't fooled. It felt like Gemma was sizing Maggie up for something, and she didn't like it one little bit. Her grip on Maggie's hand tightened.

"Hi," Maggie replied, but only because her mother had taught her good manners.

"You're just the most adorable little girl I've ever seen," Gemma said, a bright, skin-deep smile on her face. "What are you going to dress up as for Halloween."

Maggie glanced at Rosie and then back to Gemma. "I wanna be a ghost."

"Oh, but ghosts are invisible." Gemma laughed. And even though it sounded like a perfectly normal-seeming laugh, it chilled Rosie's blood. Gemma nodded at Maggie. "Powerful girls like you really ought to be *witches* for Halloween—don't you think?"

Maggie frowned and shook her head just once, stepping further back so that she was half-hidden behind Rosie.

"Sod off, Gemma," Declan said then, his voice gruff as his anger frayed the edges of his words. "We're not in the mood for your games."

Gemma held her hands up in mock surrender. "I was only saying hello," she said slyly, and then her gaze flashed back down to Maggie. "I'll let you get back to your... *family outing*." Without looking back, she took three steps away from them and disappeared into the crowd.

Rosie watched her go, glancing around the area uneasily as soon as Gemma was out of sight. She slipped an arm protectively around Maggie's shoulders, drawing her close. "Why don't we go and see about this pumpkin?" she said, glancing at Declan before ushering them towards the patch.

Rosie was caught in a whirlpool of emotions as Declan pulled his truck up in front of the cottage. Her happiness and relief at having worked things out between them was infused with her irritation at Gemma, and the pervading sense of doom brought on by the warning she and Tammy had seen in the tarot spread seemed to echo in the way Gemma had smirked at them as she had walked off. As she stepped down from the truck cab, moving aside for Maggie's usual flying-leap before tearing off towards the house clutching her pumpkin, Rosie realized that there was only really one way she *should* be feeling.

Wary.

Declan met her on the passenger side of the truck, slipping his hand around hers as they wandered up towards the porch. It was weird to know that once they reached her door he would be turning around and leaving. Gone were the days when they had bustled into the house, sorted out dinner, and then watched tv or played Go Fish all together. *Gone,* Rosie thought, *but not forgotten.* Maybe they were just gone-for-now instead.

Leaves skittered ahead of them as they went the rest of the way up the garden path, and Rosie only got to the first porch step before she felt Declan pull her back gently. She turned to look at him, squinting slightly into the bright but overcast afternoon light. Even standing on one step, he was almost a whole foot taller than she was.

"D'ya think this is private enough for smoochin'?" he asked hopefully, the corner of his mouth tilting into a cheeky half-smile. He licked his lips, glanced at the woods, and then met her gaze. "I'd hate t'be offendin' any squirrels, now."

Rosie pulled him closer, her fingertips brushing against his clipped beard as she breathed him in. The kiss was slow and soft, lingering in a way that made her wish it was possible for her to invite him inside. But the feeling of having had a near-miss with failed sex before their fight came flooding back to her, reminding her that she might not be as ready for that next step as her hormones would have her believe.

She gently broke away, letting her smaller, upturned nose rest against his larger crooked one for a moment before she licked her lips and then pressed them together resolutely. "I better go start fixin' dinner," she said gently. An almost-invitation for him to join them hung in the air, but he didn't push it.

"I'll get out of ya hair," he said gently, lifting a hand to stroke her cheek. "But first, there's somethin' I wanted to ask ya."

Rosie felt her heart quicken. "Oh?' she asked, forcing her tone to be light and fluffy.

He actually seemed *nervous*. He bit his bottom lip for a split-second, and then seemed to try and shrug it off. "I was wonderin' if you'd be interested in goin' to the Harvest ball with me?"

Rosie blinked, pleasantly surprised. "The one the church is throwing at the town hall?"

He nodded, pursing his lips in a way that tried and failed to make him look more serious.

"As friends?" One of her brows lifted at the end of her question.

"As my date," he clarified.

"Oh, I see," she breathed, deliberately teasing him. He smiled, let his huge hand fall to both of hers. The other was in his pocket. "I'll have to think about it," she smirked, leaning over to place a soft kiss to his cheek.

"Goodnight, Declan," she added, disentangling herself from him to make her way up the porch. When she glanced back over her shoulder, he was still standing at the bottom, one boot up on the top step in exactly the same position he'd used the very first night they'd met.

"Goodnight my Queen," he said, smiling gently as he watched her step inside.

# CHAPTER FOURTEEN

I t took Tammy three full days to hint boldly enough to Rosie about the kiss she had shared with Declan on the porch for Rosie to consider wanting to cough up details. The first Look she had received from her friend had been delivered over breakfast the next morning. Granola and coffee between Maggie's usual before-school chatter hadn't been enough to tempt Rosie into giving Tammy the low-down. Rosie had eventually been saved by the need to start her day, leaving Tammy to prep for her drive to Huntsville for Halloween costume sale supplies.

On Tuesday evening, a kiss on tv between two unlikely characters had been enough to prompt Tammy into throwing her a long, knowing look over the rim of her mug of hot chocolate from across the living room. Rosie had just offered her a knowing smile-and-shrug-combo, and gone back to watching the scene unfolding on the screen. But by the time the costume sale rolled around late on Wednesday afternoon, it seemed that even Tammy Holt's desire to observe the polite rules of privacy was stretched to the limit.

"I really *cannot* believe that Pastor Myles entrusted the running of the costume sale to *me*," Tammy was saying for the hundredth time since the Pastor had asked her after her guest sermon. "Me, Tammy Holt, running the annual Fall costume sale! Can you believe it! I can't! This *must* mean I have his support, don't you think?"

"It's very well deserved," Rosie replied dutifully, stuffing costumes onto hangers in an attempt to get as many ready as possible. Tammy's way of lovingly buttoning, smoothing, and then shaking out each costume before it went onto a rack just wouldn't get the job done.

"Do you think?" Tammy asked, almost completing the full conversational ritual that they had been repeating all week. "And to think that Prissy and Leanne and Marla all have to do what I say! It must mean that Pastor Myles is on my side with the Terry issue after all, don't you think?"

This last sentence was delivered in unison by Rosie, who thought the words exactly at the same time as they came out of Tammy's mouth. If it hadn't been for the memory of Declan's kiss and the promise of seeing him for the Ball to keep her going, she might not have had the patience to have the same conversation with Tammy many times over. But Tammy really was such a sweetheart that there was nothing else for it, and the next words out of her mouth were sure to give Rosie a thrill even if the previous conversation had been a little dull.

"Look Rosie," Tammy said to her friend with no small amount of satisfaction as the pair of them hung non-pagan costumes on hangers ready to be browsed through. "Declan's here."

Rosie turned her head to see the hulking Irishman cutting through the crowd towards them, and then looked back to Tammy with a smile.

Tammy huffed, and then said, "Rosie Bell, if you don't tell me what happened with that kiss on the porch I might just die from anticipation!" Her eyes were wide with expectation in a way that made Rosie bark an amused laugh.

"I wondered how long it would take you to ask!" Rosie confessed, slightly shamefaced. "You're too sweet. Okay," she hurried over to where Tammy was working on one rack of clothing, so they could be side by side. "We kissed, of course, and *then* he invited me to the Ball."

"All my *days*," Tammy sighed predictably. Then, "You said yes, didn't you?"

"Of course!" Rosie grinned, leaving just enough time for Tammy to squeal with excitement and for Declan to arrive and catch the tail end of it. He lifted his hands to his ears on reflex.

"What a soprano," he grinned, trying to cover up the fact that Tammy's squeal had almost deafened him.

She glanced between him and Rosie, and then said, "I think I'm needed by the refreshments."

Both Rosie and Declan glanced at Tammy as she took off for greener pastures, and then looked at each other. Rosie smiled shyly. "Hi."

"Hi," he replied, a genuine grin flashing across his face. Sure, he was a wall of muscle, but when he smiled, he looked infinitely more handsome. Rosie's smile widened.

"It's good to see you here," she told him, trying to ignore the butterflies in her belly. "Are you here to buy yourself a costume for the Ball?"

"Yeah" he said, glancing at the racks. He plucked a costume off the closest one, and then held it up in front of himself so that they could both view it. As luck would have it, it was a plain black pilgrim style dress, complete with a plain white cap. Declan struck a sassy pose. "Dunno that this one's really my style though."

"I wouldn't go that far," Rosie grinned, "I think you've got the calves to pull it off."

Their eyes met, and there was undeniable heat in his gaze. For a second Rosie really thought he might make some kind of dirty pun, but he seemed to stop himself at the last minute and she didn't know whether to feel relieved or disappointed.

"I'm sure I'll find something," he said, a laugh hovering on the edge of his tone as he held the dress out in front of *her*. "Ah," he smirked. "Now *that's* better, wouldn't ya agree?"

Rosie glanced down, quirked a brow. A strip of bright green material caught her eye, and she reached past him to pull a costume from the shelf. She held it up triumphantly. "I'll wear that, if you wear this."

Declan glanced down at the stereotypical leprechaun costume that was several sizes too small for him, one brow lifting in amusement. "I wouldn't even get my right arm into that," he laughed.

Rosie was about to deliver a line of her own when she noticed a deliberate movement over Declan's left shoulder. The crowd seemed to slow their movements in an almost imperceptible way, but it was plain enough to Rosie thanks to the energy shift that accompanied it.

*Witchcraft.*

And then she saw Gemma, standing in the crowd fifty of so yards away from where she was standing. The woman was just staring at the both of them, and when she managed to catch Rosie's eye a slow, knowing smirk spread over her lips. Rosie felt her breath catch in the back of her throat, and she grabbed Declan's arm— but not before the magic seemed to take a hold of her.

All she could do was stare into Gemma's eyes for what felt like an eternity, and when the spell lifted the hustle and bustle of the costume sale very nearly overwhelmed her. She gulped a breath full of air like she had been underwater for longer than she'd have liked, and that wasn't far from the truth. The influence of

Gemma's energy had felt dark and suffocating, and it was only once Rosie had broken free from the last foggy threads of it that she managed to say a single word.

"Maggie!"

"Huh?" Declan asked, raising a hand to Rosie's face in an attempt to check that she was okay. Rosie realized that he hadn't been affected by the spell. It had been meant for her. Panic gripped her heart.

"Maggie!" she insisted. "Where is she?! She was right—" she turned to where Maggie had been sitting, reading her latest book. The chair was empty.

Without a care for what she was meant to be doing or whether Declan followed or not, Rosie took off through the maze of clothes racks. "Maggie!" Her heart was thundering now, drowning out all thoughts except finding her daughter safe and sound. "*Maggie!*"

She began to tear costume hangers across the racks they were on, peering through to the next aisle as she desperately searched for her daughter. Declan had struggled to keep up with her but he was there nevertheless, looking out of breath as he peered across the parking-lot-come-costume-shop and using his height to his advantage. "Maggie!" he yelled, in a voice that was way louder than Rosie's.

There was no reply.

Several people were looking in their direction by now, and Rosie was starting to cry. Tears were stinging the back of her eyes, and she was having difficulty controlling her breathing. If anything had happened to

Maggie... oh God. She couldn't think about that. She had to keep it together. She had to find Maggie. She—

"Mom?" Maggie asked, stepping hurriedly out of one of the makeshift dressing rooms that had been constructed to the left of the rack-maze. She was wearing a costume that looked something like a cross between a cow and a scarecrow.

Rosie cried out with relief and catapulted herself towards Maggie, drawing her daughter into her arms and squeezing her tightly.

"Mom—" Maggie began to complain, before Rosie pressed several kisses to Maggie's forehead.

"I was *worried,* Pumpkin," Rosie confessed. "I thought something had happened to you."

"What are you talking about?" Maggie asked, confusion flickering over her little face. Rosie shook her head, stuffing her emotions back down.

"I just saw you weren't in the chair and I panicked," she lied smoothly, stroking Maggie's hair. "I'm sorry! I'm glad you're okay, though!" She pressed another kiss to the top of Maggie's head.

"Mom," she complained, drawing herself away and looking around at the crowd, who had mostly gone back about their business with the exception of a few of the Church kids who were looking on eagerly. "Ix-nay on the issing-kay."

Maggie stepped back into the change room to get dressed in her own clothes again. Declan leaned close to Rosie, his hands on her upper arms as he pressed a quick kiss to her temple. "You wanna fill me in?" he asked in a low voice before straightening.

"Gemma," Rosie murmured darkly. "I saw her here."

Declan glanced behind him warily, and then ran a hand down Rosie's arm. "Where?"

Rosie nodded her chin in the direction she'd seen the woman, so she didn't have to point and draw attention. Declan nodded in return and moved away. "I'll go check it out. You stay here with Maggie."

Rosie took a deep breath, trying to still her thundering heart. By the time Maggie got out of the changing room with the arm full of costumes she had taken in with her, Declan was back. He shook his head silently.

"I should get Maggie home," Rosie said. She wouldn't quite get her heart under control until they were home safe within her wards.

"Wait," Declan stopped her. "What time should I pick you up for the ball?"

Rosie hesitated. She didn't want to make Declan feel badly, but every time Gemma had made a move against Maggie, it was when they were both with him. She tucked a lock of hair behind her ear.

"Actually, why don't I just meet you there?" she offered.

He swallowed, staring at her hard for a couple of moments, but then nodded. "If that's what you want," he told her. He glanced between Rosie and Maggie, before his gaze lingered on the first. "I'll see you at the ball, then," he nodded. "G'night, Miss Maggie."

She watched him walk away with a pang of disappointment. She hated his thinking this was what she wanted. It *wasn't* what she wanted. It was what she needed in order to keep her daughter safe. Because one thing was certain.

She didn't trust Gemma farther than she could throw her.

# CHAPTER FIFTEEN

T he night of the Harvest Ball was eerily quiet.
Rosie stood on a rocky outcrop above The
Ridge, looking down at the township
of Mosswood sitting breathless in anticipation beside
the winding Chickasaw River below. She took a few
deep breaths while she admired the view. For all that the
townsfolk weren't always her cup of tea, it *was* a
gorgeous place.

She must have stood watching for a good while,
because the sun had snuck closer to the horizon before
she'd realized what was happening. As the first rays
touched the mountains on the west side of the river,
Rosie gave up her perch and went inside to get ready.
Maggie was thrilled with the plain, classic 'ghost'
costume she had gotten from the sale. She was already
dressed, sitting on the couch watching tv through
the black mesh holes Tammy had sewn into

the white sheet that covered her and sipping what Rosie seriously suspected was a Yoohoo chocolate milk where her mother couldn't see.

Rosie stepped into her room, glancing at the black pilgrim costume that Declan had picked out for her waiting on a hanger hooked onto her dresser. She didn't know what had possessed her to buy it, except to get a laugh out of Declan, but now she was stuck with it. Rosie pulled the dress on over her head, pleased with the way the top fit but annoyed at the long sleeves and the long, unshapely skirt. It didn't fit her mood at all, and she stared forlornly at her reflection in her mirror.

She needed help.

Tammy was humming in the kitchen and drying some dishes, dressed in a black dress that accentuated her curves to perfection. A translucent poncho covered the dress, printed with iridescent blues, deep purples, and shimmering silvers all delineated by thick black lines that resembled the pattern of a butterfly's wings. She looked fantastic, even though it wasn't a costume that Rosie would have gone for herself. It was predictably modest but had a fun and flirty quality to it that surprised Rosie.

"You look amazing," she cooed at Tammy, genuinely pleased for her friend.

Tammy glanced at Rosie over her shoulder, a bashful smile lighting up her rounded face. "Aw, thanks hon! You look—" she paused midway through returning the compliment, and then petered off as she turned around to face Rosie properly. "Um, you look—very..."

Rosie couldn't help but smile at how polite Tammy was striving to be. "Unshapely?" she supplied helpfully.

Tammy sagged with relief once she knew that she wasn't going to put her foot in her mouth. "Gosh, I'm sorry, but *yeah*," she sighed, shaking her head as she took in the full effect of dress that was tight across Rosie's bust and then baggy everywhere else. The sleeves hung down in what could almost be described as a Morticia Addams styled affair—if Morticia Addams' wore disfigured bat wing sleeves that looked more nun's habit than sexy seductress.

Rosie laughed, flapping her 'wings' for effect. Tammy let herself giggle too, and reached for an open bottle of wine to pour them both a glass.

"What are we gonna do about it, then?" she asked Rosie, surveying the situation more closely. "I have my sewing machine in the car. I can take the bodice in here," she grabbed a few inches of fabric from Rosie's waist, "Maybe do something with the sleeves.'"

Rosie nodded gratefully. "I'd be thrilled to make it something a little more... well. *Sexy*," she admitted, making Tammy both blush and grin.

"Sexy how?"

An idea flew into Rosie's brain, taking up residence in her creative belfry. "What about a sexy *witch*? It would be really fun! We need to work with this black dress, and it seems an easy way out."

Tammy seemed to consider it, and grinned. "It *would* be fun to make something that didn't go all the way to the floor once in a little while," she agreed.

Rosie grinned and topped up their wine glasses.

The much shorter skirt of Rosie's dress fluttered around her thighs as she, Tammy, and Maggie made their way toward Town Hall. Tammy had worked a miracle on her dress, which now had short puffy sleeves held up by hair ties, crisscrossing black lace over the white bodice, and a witchy styled bat hem that was well above the knee. They had even used excess material from her skirt to cover a quick witch's hat, that was really just a cone and a flat circle made out of an empty cereal box. Recyclables or no, Rosie felt like a million bucks.

Maggie raced ahead as usual. Rosie was excited that her daughter was excited, but she hadn't forgotten the look in Gemma's face at the costume sale, or the chill right down her spine that had accompanied it. Tammy floated across the street beside her, the filmy wings of her costume fanning out with the movement.

Rosie was pleased to admit that the decorating committee hadn't failed. The door to the Hall was framed by a huge straw archway, beset with intricate arrangements of fall leaves and pinecones. Pumpkins sat strategically at the base, carved with a variety of non-pagan images and symbols that glowed thanks to the battery-operated candles inside. The inside of the building was just as good. Gentle candlelight filled the cavernous hall, held aloft by nearly invisible fishing line to look like the candles were floating. A ghost 'band' that Rosie suspected was just a bunch of mannequins from the local thrift store covered in sheets 'played' Halloween hits on the stage at the back of the room. It wasn't quite magic, but it was definitely magical.

"Tammy Holt, just the woman I need!" a familiar voice gushed to their left. All three of them turned to see the Pastor rushing over, hands outstretched, as though he had had seen his salvation—which was ironic, because he was dressed to look like Jesus Christ.

Tammy blinked, took in the costume, and then a wide grin spread across her face. "Pastor Myles!" she exclaimed, flushing when he took her hand warmly. "Isn't that costume a little... blasphemous?" she whispered.

The pastor leaned forward a little conspiratorially. "I think it might actually be more blasphemous *not* to invite the Savior to our pagan celebration, don't you think?" He grinned, and then paused to take in the sight of Tammy's costume, and added, "You're a vision."

For a brief moment, the two looked at each other with such focus that Rosie wondered if she shouldn't give them some privacy, but then Myles snapped out of it. He gestured hurriedly toward a nearby refreshment table. "I need your help with the snacks. I'm afraid that Leanne mixed up the non-peanut peanut butter cups with the *real* peanut butter cups!"

Tammy gasped. "But, allergies!"

"Exactly," the Pastor shook his head seriously. "Can I count on you?"

"Of course!" Tammy agreed immediately. 'Leave it to me!"

"Mom," Maggie interrupted, bored by the adult drama that Rosie was so entertained by. "Can I go hang out with Amy, Jesse, and the other kids?"

"As long as I can see you at all times—yes."

Maggie barely had time to reply with "Deal!" before she was making her way across the hall to where the other kids were starting to congregate by the stage. Rosie followed Tammy over to the snack table, where Tammy began rapidly dividing the mass of homemade peanut butter cups into two groups.

"Those look exactly the same to me," Rosie frowned, leaning in for a better look. "How do you know which is which? Does the non-peanut peanut butter look less waxy or something?"

Tammy raised a brow and looked at her friend.

"No," she said slowly, smiling. "The peanut ones are in the blue cases, the others are in the red ones. The Pastor's just colorblind."

"Oh," Rosie said with a smile, relieved that it wasn't about some kind of domestic voodoo that she would never be able to perform. She got to work, and somehow ended up helping Tammy host the entire event. It must have been an hour before the refreshment tables were to Tammy's liking, and Rosie almost hesitated to mention the punch bowl, which was looking like a beach at low tide.

"We're almost out of punch," she said to Tammy, who nodded.

"We'd better hop on over to the kitchen and grab some more fixin's," she agreed. "Can you give me a hand? We'll need a whole box full of juice cartons to fill up that bowl, plus fruit besides."

Rosie glanced around until she could see Maggie in her ghost costume, and then nodded back at Tammy. "Of course," she agreed.

She followed Tammy through the crowd towards the Hall's kitchen. It really was a grand old building. The columns they passed in the halls made it seem much fancier than a town like Mosswood deserved. They ducked down a less-fancy hallway, and the sound of something metal clattering to the floor made them both look up in concern. Tammy recovered first. She propelled herself forward and pushed on the swinging kitchen door, gasping loudly in shock when she could see what had made the racket. Rosie rushed to her side, and then gasped herself.

A large metal bowl of popcorn was spilled all over the tiles, which explained the noise. But the shocking part was that Prissy Bishop was spread across the stainless-steel commercial kitchen counter. She was dressed as an angel, with fluffy white feathered wings and a golden halo on wires bobbing above her head. Her white flowing dress was hiked up around her waist and her legs were in the air—held in place by a huge red deer with fake antlers.

Terry was still grunting and going for gold, not yet having realized that he and his mistress had an audience. Prissy let out short bursts of breathy little 'Oh!'s with each thrust, and it wasn't until the door swung closed behind both Tammy and Rosie that Prissy tilted her head back to look—and then scream.

Terry's head snapped up and—seeing his wife—he pulled out and covered himself up so fast that Rosie hoped he got himself caught in his zipper. Prissy scrambled off the table, her dress falling to provide her with some modesty but not hiding the white sparkly thong that was laying abandoned on the tiles a few feet away. Tammy looked at the underwear for a long moment, and then her burning gaze fixed itself on Prissy.

"Tammy!" Prissy cried in a shrill voice. "Please! This isn't what it looks like!"

"I reckon you're right," Tammy said, her face

frighteningly calm. "Because what it looks like is my husband and my best friend preachin' to me about forgivin' and forgettin', when they're busy *forgettin' about the sanctity of marriage!*" Tammy threw one of Prissy's lines right back at her, making Rosie want to erupt with a cheer.

"You don't understand," Prissy continued, leaving Terry to shrink as far into the background as he could.

"And I don't want to," Tammy said with a harsh laugh. "Now I know why you were so desperate for me to stay with my no-good, cheatin' husband! It was to cover up your own sin!" Tammy shook her head, anger and sadness and hurt all plain as day on her face. "I wonder if Myles will feel like forgiving or forgetting?"

"Please Tammy!" Prissy said then, rushing forward. "Please don't tell Myles! It would ruin him."

All of the emotions in Tammy's expression melted into pure disgust. "No, Priscilla," she said, stepping forward to grab the box holding the cartons of juice. "It'll only ruin *you.*"

"Terry's here too!" Prissy countered, now trying to shift the blame. "It's not like I have done this on my own!"

"I don't give a rat's red derrière what Terry does anymore," Tammy shrugged.

She turned to Rosie, nodding at the fruit basket nearby. "Can you grab that please, Rosie?"

Rosie picked up the basket and stopped on the way out the door to look back at the pathetic creatures stood huddled together on the other side of the island counter. She looked them both up and down scathingly.

"Hallelujah," she said with relief, before following Tammy back to the party.

Tammy plonked the box of juice cartons on the table. She took one carton, shaking it vigorously in a way that would have made a grown man squirm—it looked like she might like to catch hold of Terry's neck and do the same to him. And Rosie wouldn't blame her. Catching your man in the act with another woman was one thing; catching him with someone you had considered a friend was another. Adding the fact that Prissy had been trying to talk Tammy into *keeping* Terry only made it that much worse.

If it had been Rosie in this predicament, she didn't think she would have been strangling a juice carton.

"You okay, hon?" She asked Tammy. Her friend barked a mirthless laugh.

"Peachy," she replied, and Rosie could have kicked herself for asking such a stupid question. Tammy poured the juice into the punch bowl, and then caught hold of another carton to throttle. She looked up, and suddenly she seemed even more flustered. Rosie followed her gaze to where Pastor Myles was coming towards them through the crowd, a wide smile on his handsome face.

"Will you tell him?" Rosie asked, genuinely wondering how this was all likely to play out now. So far there hadn't been any sign of Prissy or Terry emerging from the kitchen, which must have only served to make Tammy madder.

Tammy shook her head slightly, looking down to the punch for a moment. "I won't have to," she said, glancing up at Rosie who frowned slightly. But then a flurry of white appeared, and Prissy met Myles in front of the refreshment table before he had a chance to congratulate Tammy on her excellent punch-making skills. Rosie took a deep breath, so that she could hold it for the duration of what promised to be an epic showdown.

"Darlin'!" Prissy cried, trying to be as dramatic as possible but keep her voice as low as possible so as not to attract undue attention. "She's lying—she doesn't know what she saw! Please, forgive me!"

Myles frowned from beneath his Jesus costume, the crinkles of his forehead visible even if the down-turning of his mouth wasn't. He glanced at Tammy and Rosie, and then at Terry who had come to an abrupt halt behind Prissy as he had chased after her across the dance floor.

"Terry doesn't mean *anythin'* to me," Prissy went on, clasping her husband's hands desperately. "Satan took hold of me, is what it was! I need you to lift me up in prayer!"

Myles now tore his eyes away from his wife and looked to Terry. No amount of red face paint or fake antlers could hide the guilt written plainly across Terry's face, and realization began to dawn on Myles'. He looked back at Prissy, his eyes suddenly dark with anger, just as she tilted her face up to him with large, puppy-dog eyes and a pout that must have cost a fortune in lip-filler.

"What would Jesus do?" she asked her husband, stepping her hands over the top of his as though inviting him to join with her in prayer. But when Myles pulled his hands from her grip and set his shoulders, Rosie knew that it didn't bode well for Prissy *or* Terry.

"I can't claim to know what the real Jesus would do in this situation," Myles said, barely containing his anger. "But *this* Jesus would do… this!!"

It was strange to watch Jesus lay a killer right hook, but that's exactly what happened. Myles' fist connected perfectly with Terry's left jaw, sending him reeling through the crowd. People scattered to make way for the stumbling dude holding his mouth and turned to see Myles advancing.

"Myles, no!" Prissy squealed, making everyone who wasn't already looking turn around to see what the commotion was all about.

"The hell'd ya do that for?" Terry spluttered, spitting onto the floor in a way that demonstrated just how uncouth he really was. The crowd had formed around them in a ring by now, with many folk jumping to see their upstanding preacher looking a little wild as the rest of them did when not under his careful ministration.

"Lord knows you've had this comin'," Myles growled, pulling his fist back.

Terry tried to duck but wasn't quick enough; he copped another blow to his left cheek that made his head snap back and then forward again. He bent forward, hands pressed to his face, as he leaned against the refreshment table for support. "Now, hold on—" he huffed, trying to catch his breath. "You're a man of God, ain't ya?"

Indecision flickered across Myles' face, and he softened slightly. "You're right," he said, holding his hands up to signal that he was done with the fight. "We need to settle this like men, Terry. I—"

But he didn't get to finish what he was going to say. Terry lunged forward like a viper. He gripped the Tupperware platter that had been holding the peanut butter cups, sending them flying through the air and into the crowd as he smashed the platter straight into Myles's face.

"Take *that,* ya holier-than-thou sumbitch!" Terry crowed. Myles stumbled back, hands pressed to his nose, and the crowd gasped.

It was on like Donkey Kong. Myles sprang forward, hands outstretched for Terry like he might just strangle him the way Tammy had been strangling juice cartons. He was thinner and sprightlier than Terry, and though Terry had started to run Myles caught him easily. He jumped on Terry's back and wrapped an arm across the front of his chest, and for a few seconds it looked like Jesus was riding a giant deer across the room. Though in reality it was just an ass.

Terry had the weight advantage. He gripped Myles' arm with both hands and leaned forward, obviously trying to flip the Pastor over his shoulder and onto the hard-wooden floor. Both men lost their balance and tumbled to the ground in a flurry of false beards and brown face paint. They rolled over and over, each fighting to come out on top, but neither of them doing much *fighting* besides that.

Terry grabbed hold of Myles' wig, yanking it off savagely. Myles placed his hand over Terry's face and pushed, trying to get some space from the other man before Terry saw his opportunity and sank his teeth into the side of Myles' hand.

The Pastor howled like a wolf, ripping his hand back and then throwing it forward straight into Terry's nose. There was a sickening crunch, and a spurt of blood. Myles rocked back onto his heels as though he couldn't believe what he had done, and Terry saw that as his chance to escape. He stumbled to his feet and made to take off through the crowd—but not before Myles realized what he was doing. He leapt to his feet and charged after Terry, the crowd separating to let them through.

They ran almost a whole lap of the room, which gave Tammy time to step out from behind the refreshments table. She was carrying the bowl of half-made punch she had been working on, and as Terry came around the bend again, she dumped it right over her husband's head, bowl and all. Terry slipped on the wetness and landed flat on his backside, the punch bowl careening around his head like a horseshoe on a stake. The crowd cheered.

Myles walked up slowly behind the conquered Terry, barely able to catch his breath. Terry pushed the bowl off his head and stood in a rush, staring down his pastor with venom.

"Terry Holt," Myles said, breathing hard but looking as if he was done with this fight, "You're a liar, a cheater, and an adulterer, and you're lacking God in your life."

"Well," Terry said, taking a step backward, "at least I can make your wife come."

Myles froze. The crowd gasped. Rosie thought Myles was going to level the hunter, but he never got the chance, because Tammy did it for him.

"Funny," she interrupted, hands on her hips, "you never could yours."

Whistles and jeers went up from the crowd and Terry sneered, but knew when he was beaten. He turned on his heel and tried to march off, but the floor where his wife had dunked him was still wet, and his marching was robbed of all its power by his nearly busting his ass again.

"Darlin'?" Prissy said, interjecting just as soon as it was safe enough to do so. She tried to approach her husband, lifting her hands as though to touch his face. Myles lifted his own hands to stop her touching him and took several steps away from her.

"I am not now, nor will I ever again be, your darlin'," he told his wife plainly.

Prissy gasped, crocodile tears in her eyes, as she turned and fled from the party, trailing a cloud of dramatic sobs behind her.

The crowd began to disperse, moving off to gossip in small groups about bearing witness to their Pastor going Old Testament on a member of the congregation. Myles wiped his face across the wide sleeve of his Jesus costume, snatched his wig up off the floor and turned to Tammy.

"I'm sorry they did that to you, Tammy," he said, still catching his breath.

"Myles," she replied gently, "they did it to you, too."

Confusion scrunched up the pastor's face, but then he seemed to decide what to do with it. He gave Tammy a straight-lipped smile and wandered off into the hallway. Tammy watched him go, her eyes large and her lips pursed. Rosie looked between them both, before laying a hand on Tammy's shoulder.

"Why don't you go see if he's okay," she suggested

gently. "That was intense, and I bet he could use a friend. Plus..." Rosie shrugged slightly, "you're both in this together, it seems."

Tammy nodded, sighing at the sight of the destroyed refreshment table.

Rosie watched Tammy leave and then started to clean up the mess surrounding her as best she could. She couldn't believe that Myles had just had a fight with Terry in front of the whole congregation. Just when she had started hoping that the drama would settle down, life seemed to have other ideas. She wished that she had someone here with her to debrief with, but she hadn't seen Declan all night and Tammy was busy with Myles. Maybe it was the perfect time to check in with Maggie.

Maggie's costume had made it easy for Rosie to spot her throughout the evening, thanks to the portable black lights that had been installed around the Hall for the event. A neon-blue ghost was an easy mark, and Rosie could see exactly where her daughter was standing, towards the back of a group of kids who were having some kind of dance-off.

"Maggie!" She called across the crowd. Maggie didn't turn, so Rosie cupped her hands around her mouth so that her voice would carry. "*Maggie!*"

Maggie didn't turn around, so Rosie cut through the crowd until she was within reaching instance. "Hey," she said, reaching out a hand to place on Maggie's shoulder. "How's it going over—"

Her words and thoughts abandoned her as the sheet

that had been covering her daughter fell to the ground, revealing nothing but empty air beneath it. Where the hell was Maggie? How long had she been keeping a watchful eye on a floating sheet in the crowd? Her skin burst out in goosebumps.

Maggie—her beautiful, gorgeous child— was missing.

# CHAPTER SIXTEEN

Rosie burst into the kitchen for the second time that evening, with even less fucks to give for anyone's privacy than she'd had the first time around. Tammy and Myles were standing close together, with Tammy pressing a dish cloth full of ice cubes to the bridge of Myles' nose. They both jumped when Rosie came in, and Myles shifted a respectful distance from Tammy and took over holding his own ice pack.

"Tammy, Maggie's missing. I've checked the inside of the building, and I can't find her anywhere. I think —" Rosie's voice choked up before she could finish her sentence.

Tammy must have heard the sob behind her words, because she reached out to place a hand on Rosie's shoulder as they galloped towards the entrance.

"Don't worry," she promised, "We'll find her. She might have just stepped outside for some air."

"I hope so," Rosie worried, unsure how to explain a floating sheet. There were a few people milling out on the street—largely people who smoked popping out for a cigarette with their compatriots. Rosie didn't care that she had apparently entered Marlboro Country; her only desire was to see a familiar head of dark, glossy hair and hear Maggie's laugh as she chatted to her friends. She was granted neither.

And then she saw Declan, leprechaun costume in place, throwing some full trash bags into a dumpster. So he'd been waylaid to volunteer for the event, too. He took a moment to appreciate her own costume before their eyes locked, and she could tell by the serious look that came over his face that he realized something was amiss. He was by her side in a heartbeat, bending down to look into her face.

"What's wrong?" he asked, the question full of concern. His eyes searched hers, and his hand came up to cup her cheek lightly. "What's happened?"

"What's happened," Rosie snapped, her panic replaced by anger that found an outlet now that Declan was here, "is that fucking *Gemma* has kidnapped Maggie!"

"Gemma?" Tammy asked, stunned.

"What?" He looked blankly from Rosie to Tammy, and back again.

"Where'd you see her last?"

"Inside—about twenty minutes ago... I think," Rosie added. "I found her costume, but no Maggie."

"Where could she have gone?" Tammy asked. "Do you think she might have gone home? We could check that out first, just to make sure?"

And then a memory hit Rosie. A memory of a dark clearing in the woods, where not even the grass would grow. A place where a black tone altar had tasted bitter blood but was still thirsty for more.

She looked up at Declan.

"The dead clearing," she said, knowing within her heart that it was exactly where she would find her daughter. But would they be too late? "We have to hurry!" she demanded.

Declan, sensing the urgency, looked around them. The small black Smart car belonging to Maude from the Beep'n Sleep was parked on the side of the road, and there were no other cars in sight.

"Come on," he said stiffly, placing his hand in the small of Rosie's back and directing her across the street. "I drove Maude here, so I have her keys.

"You can't be serious," she said, torn between needing to get to the other side of town at the speed of light and not knowing how on earth Declan would even fold himself *into* that car. "We'll be packed in there like sardines."

"We don't have a choice," he said. Rosie felt the now-familiar rush of him gathering his energy. By the time the three of them reached the car, it was unlocked.

"I'm drivin'," Tammy announced, scooting over to

the driver's side. "I've lived in this town my whole life, an' I know these roads better'n either of y'all."

"Fair call," Declan agreed, handing her the keys. He sat on the front passenger seat and then scrunched his legs inside before looking up at Rosie, who was still standing on the pavement. He patted his lap. "Hop on."

If the situation hadn't been so serious, Rosie might have laughed. "Don't be ridiculous!"

"It's the only way we're getting' up there," Declan told her, "and we don't have time to argue about it."

Damn it, he was right. Rosie turned to park her butt in his lap, her cheeks burning. She'd been close enough to him plenty of times, but this was just plain embarrassing. She managed to fit her legs between his, but her head was pressed hard up against the roof and she had to slouch uncomfortably towards Tammy so that he could close the door. The partygoers on the street watched them with incredulous expressions as the car tore off, taking a sharp right onto Main Street.

"Where exactly are we goin'?" Tammy asked, ignoring the fact that Declan had one knee poking through the space between her seat and Rosie's.

"We need to go past the cottage, further up the track into Needlepoint Woods," Rosie instructed. "We need to get to a clearing that's deeper into the woods."

"Okay," Tammy said. "There's a bit of a look-out by some rocks up that way, which has an area that's kind of a parking lot of sorts. A lover's lane type place. That's as far as we can take the car."

Tammy planted her foot. They zoomed through town past the Elementary school, the engine of the car sounding like a wound-up rubber band that was ready to snap. It was more Vespa than Mustang, but the three of them kept their faces stern and their minds determined as they took the corner that would lead up The Ridge towards Fox Cottage.

"Can't this thing go any faster?" Declan asked impatiently as they slowed considerably going up the hill.

"It's going as fast as it can with a giant leprechaun weighing it down," Tammy retorted through gritted teeth.

Rosie had to admit that the crawling pace of the car wasn't doing much for her nerves either. She gathered her energy, holding it inside the space between her lungs and the bottom of her rib cage. "Maybe try shifting down a gear," she said to Tammy, who obliged. As soon as the gear dropped back, Rosie began to release her energy.

The car scooted up the hill, propelled by Rosie's magic. Tammy blinked and gripped the wheel, looking pleased with herself. "There she goes!" She announced. Rosie caught Declan's eye in the rear-view mirror, and he gave her a tight but appreciative smile.

With the added oomph from Rosie's magic, the little car-that-could made it to the lookout parking lot in record time. The three of them piled out of the vehicle like clowns from a circus car.

"We have to hurry," Rosie urged them, breaking into a dead run as she made a beeline for the thick expanse of woods beyond the parking lot. Anyone who couldn't keep up now would have to follow at their own pace; she wasn't willing to risk Maggie's safety on waiting for people. She began to crash through the underbrush, hearing Declan's heavy footsteps behind her. She dashed through the curtain of Spanish moss that had seemed so beautiful in the light of the full moon but which was now just a hindrance.

Declan caught hold of her hand before she could go any further, using all his strength to pull her to a forcible stop. She could hear Tammy struggling to catch up with them and whirled to face him.

"We have to be smart about this," he murmured to her. "If Gemma hears us coming through the forest like bulls at a gate, who knows what she'll do."

Rosie hated that he was right. It was *her child* in the clutches of whatever the hell Gemma was now— because she wasn't human. She wasn't just a witch. Not anymore. The raging mama bear inside of her wanted to storm into that clearing, take back her cub and make Gemma pay for all the damage she'd caused. But she knew that she had to be better than that.

For Maggie's sake.

Rosie nodded just once, and Declan took the lead. Rosie waited until Tammy's eyes met hers across the expanse of dark forest. She pressed one finger to her lips in a 'shush'ing gesture, and then nodded after Declan before she followed him.

They crept toward the clearing together, grimacing every time their feet snapped a twig or crunched on leaves that could give away their location. And then a long, gut-wrenching cry filled the night air. A flock of birds were startled from their perch in one of the trees and they crashed through branches as they took to the sky, squawking indignantly.

Rosie strained to stop herself from running towards that cry. She almost gave in, her body tensing as she prepared to bolt towards her child when Declan grabbed her hand.

"That was Gemma," he whispered, before voices drifted to them through the darkness.

"Please! It's the only way!" Gemma was wheezing, sounding like she was out of breath. Her British accent, usually crisp, was sounding more East London than South Kensington. "I'll die otherwise. Your mother wouldn't help me, because she was jealous of my relationship with Declan."

"I don't believe you!" Maggie declared. "If you were gonna die, she would help you—I know she would! My Mom is a good person!"

Rosie's heart melted, while her hatred of Gemma solidified. What on earth was she trying to do to Maggie?

"It's the truth, whether you believe it or not,"

Gemma gasped. "My world grows dark, child. I need you to do it. *Now*."

Declan, Rosie, and Tammy continued to creep through the woods closer to the voices. As they moved, the atmosphere changed noticeably. The branches on the trees were dead and dry, hanging at odd angles like broken limbs. The underbrush became scraggly and then dry, as though the life had been sucked right out of it. And the air was thicker, almost like tar that wanted to invade their lungs and then smother them.

There was a silence before Maggie spoke again.

"Are you *really* dying?"

Rosie felt her adrenaline surge even higher, now that it sounded like Maggie might give in to Gemma's wiles. She couldn't hold herself back any longer. She pushed past Declan, who tried and failed to catch her.

"Yessss," Gemma hissed. "Thisss will only sssting a little..."

It was no longer the smooth aristocratic voice belonging to the woman. Now it was the sly rasp of something that should never have been released to the plane they were all living on.

"Okay then," Maggie said, fear tinging her voice.

Rosie crashed through the last of the bushes just in time to see Gemma pressing Maggie down onto the altar, bending over with her mouth open. She held a ceremonial-looking dagger in one hand, and Maggie's throat in the other.

"*Magnolia!*" Rosie screamed. Her voice rang

through the clearing like a church bell chiming on Easter Sunday. Gemma's glamour flickered and then failed completely, revealing her true self.

She was no longer the elegant, lithe British witch that had been a thorn in Rosie's side. She was hunched, her limbs twisted like the aged branches of a tree that grew in soil with too much salt. Her face was twisted too; a grotesque landscape full of boils, and sagging skin that jiggled independently of bodily movement. But the worst part was her eyes. They were black, and flat, and dead-looking. They reminded Rosie of a shark's eyes, and she suddenly had a vision of Gemma rolling them back in her head while she sank her yellow, broken teeth into poor Maggie's young flesh.

There was no fucking way she would let that happen.

Maggie screamed and began to struggle, but Gemma's grip was too strong. Rosie started to run across the clearing, gathering her magic. She could hear Declan doing the same behind her.

Maggie writhed on the altar, held fast by Gemma who looked up at Declan, Rosie, and Tammy and grinned.

"Too late," she sang, holding up the dagger in her other hand and wiggling it at them mockingly. A dark smudge of blood strained the blade.

"Once I take this child'sss blood into myssself, the Line of Prophecy will flow through my veinsss! *I* will be the fated Queen of the Lossst!"

"Fuck *that!*" Declan cried, hot on Rosie's heels.

Maggie strained to look over at her mother, an expression of fear and relief on her little face. It was as though Rosie's presence gave her a strength she hadn't realized she possessed. Within a heartbeat, a huge pulse of energy burst forth from Maggie, accompanied by a blinding light. Rosie shielded her eyes for a moment but didn't stop running.

As the light died down, she noticed that Gemma had been knocked backwards by the force and was lying on the ground beside the altar. The dagger had flown out of her hand, glinting dangerously from the dirt a few feet away from her. Declan changed direction and headed for the dagger, while Rosie pressed on towards Maggie.

Gemma's eyes flicked between the both of them, as though she were summing up the bigger risk. The moment she decided, her dark eyes shone with an oil-slick gleam, not unlike a cat's in a flash of light. She reached out, her magic bubbling up in the air around her. With an animalistic cry, she released it towards Declan.

"Watch out!" Rosie yelled.

He looked up so that he could dodge whatever was headed his way. Diving forward he executed a neat commando roll, leaving Gemma's spell to fizzle into the darkness beyond him. She howled with frustration.

Rosie skidded to a halt on the dry dirt, deciding to take Gemma on. Tammy bolted past her, eyes wide as she looked at the space where Gemma's magic had been. She was at Maggie's side within seconds.

Rosie held her hands out and then pushed them forward, her own magic sizzling and white-hot as it coursed across the clearing to hit Gemma. She screamed for a moment but then activated some kind of forcefield around herself that expanded, dark red and glowing.

"Everyone!" Declan roared, "*get down!*"

Tammy pulled Maggie off the altar, and they both shielded themselves behind it. Rosie and Declan hit the dirt, just in time for thousands of tiny fireballs to spray like bullets out of the energy field surrounding Gemma. She cackled inside, standing and lifting her gnarled hands triumphantly. But her laughter was cut short when a dazzling yellow bolt of energy hit her protective shield, making it shudder.

Declan stood not too far away, his magic focused on breaking the forcefield. Rosie joined him in a heartbeat, harnessing her own power and throwing it into the mix. Her magic was a radiant blue that filled the other side of Gemma's energy field. The magic became a bright, iridescent green where the edges met as it completely engulfed Gemma.

The forcefield shuddered again as though it might break, and then it was gone. Elation flooded Rosie and then was gone just as quickly, as a sizzling red lightning bolt shot towards Declan.

"*No!*" she screamed, but it was too late.

Complacency had been the chink in his armor and the bolt hit him square in the chest. Panic washed over his face as he realized what was happening; his legs stopped being able to move, and he lost motor function from his feet moving upward.Slowly, inch by inch, he became a statue sculpted from the same dark rock that the altar was made out of.

Rosie beat back the panic that threatened to engulf her. It would do no one she loved any good. She turned on the hag, fury burning deep within her soul.

"There," Gemma smirked, dusting off her hands so that her long talons clicked together. "Now it'sss jussst usss girlsss..."

Rosie screamed and threw another bolt of energy at Gemma, but the other woman blocked it and then countered. The red lightning hit Rosie and zapped her energy away from her, and Rosie realized that Gemma had stolen the rest of Declan's energy when she'd turned him to stone. Rosie fell to her knees, glancing towards Maggie and Tammy out of the corner of her eye. She could see Maggie twist away from Tammy and run for the blade, Tammy taking off after her. She wanted to yell at them both to run, but she was so tired... so *sleepy*.

"I knew you weren't ssstrong enough for Declan," Gemma hissed, sounding more smug than ever. "Jussst a little wassste of ssspace. And ssso easssy to put out of your misssery..."

The sound of Gemma building her energy was

almost deafening. It held all the dangerous thrum of a nuclear reactor at overload capacity, and if Rosie hadn't already been almost ready to lie down in defeat the sound alone would have brought her to her knees. She could hardly hold her eyes open. She saw one last, devilish smile on Gemma's face before releasing the spell that would undoubtedly be the end of her.

But then Maggie was there. At the very last moment, a little hand slipped into hers as her daughter stood tall and faced Gemma herself. The bolt of magic meant to end Rosie hit Maggie instead. It enveloped her in dark, red magic as thick as blood, covering every inch of her. Maggie's grip on Rosie's hand fell away, and Rosie felt her heart fall out of her chest right along with it. Maggie collapsed on the dirt in front of her, and Rosie only just saw Gemma fall to the ground—spent—as she fell forward to cover her child's body with hers.

Maggie was still breathing... but only just. Rosie didn't have enough magic left to save her the way she had saved Declan after their showdown with Randy, and she knew it. Despair started to fill her heart as the reality of the situation began to dawn on her, but a flicker of movement near Gemma momentarily stole her attention.

Tammy stood over Gemma, the dagger raised above her head as though she intended to plunge it down into the hag. Rosie's eyes widened and she opened her mouth to scream. With Maggie's blood still on the blade, stabbing Gemma now would be giving her exactly what she had wanted all along! But she was too late.

Tammy's face was contorted in pain and rage. She gripped the dagger tightly.

"Devil take you, cause I sure don't want you where I'm going!" she cried, before she sank to her knees and plunged the dagger deep into Gemma's chest.

Rosie felt the world fall out from under her. Maggie, Declan... nothing could be done to save them, or even herself. She fell back onto her butt in the dirt, clutching Maggie weakly with tears streaming openly down her face.

Tammy was staring at Gemma, unable to believe what she had just done. She backed away, holding her trembling hands out in front of her. Her eyes were wide as saucers, and her lips moved silently, as though she were praying.

Gemma was making a wet, gurgling sound as she lay still on the ground. Rosie could feel the transition starting to take place. Little pops of energy sparked from Gemma's body, signaling her blood mixing with Maggie's. Rosie watched helplessly as the last of her magic began to combine itself with Gemma's. The chain reaction continued until the magical force within Gemma set a glowing aura around the place where Tammy had stabbed her.

Her heart.

But Gemma looked more than half dead from magical exhaustion. As the blood pact started to gain momentum, it soaked up the last reserves of Gemma's magic. The aura around her heart flickered, dimming to a tiny flicker before it exploded into a brilliant white light that lit up the whole of the clearing. Without enough magic left to sustain the blood pact, Maggie's blood had been Gemma's undoing instead of the power trip she had wanted it to be.

"Praise the Lord!" Tammy gasped, shielding her eyes from the blinding light. Rosie barely had enough strength to turn her head away, her eyes falling to Maggie's blank face. Her eyelashes were so perfect, resting serenely against her little cheeks...

And then the sizzling began. It was a strange, unnatural sound not unlike the noise a boiling kettle makes when there's water trapped underneath it. As the bright light faded, Rosie could see the ground crumbling from beneath Gemma's body. And then the ground began to sink around her. The dirt seemed to creep over her, covering her sagging flesh. Thin tree roots snaked up to grasp at her arms and legs, pulling her down into the soil where nature could claim her bones and neutralize the evil she had created within herself.

"Well butter my butt and call me a biscuit," Tammy marveled, before turning to look at Rosie. She took one look at her friend's face, and then the limp body of Maggie in her lap and scrambled towards them both.

"Call an ambulance," Rosie begged. "I don't know if she's gonna make it."

Rosie lay back on the dirt, breathing hard in an

attempt to stop her grief from overwhelming her. A breeze whispered through the clearing as though consoling her. It carried with it the sweet scents of the summer that had just passed; fresh grass and lemonade, and Rosie took a huge lungful of it as she tried to stay strong. But she felt her mind was slipping away from her. The ground suddenly seemed softer and more forgiving, and the air was cleansed of its thick oppressive atmosphere. Rosie lay a hand to the dirt beneath her and felt fresh shoots of soft grass there instead.

She tilted her head to the left and saw that the dead trees surrounding the clearing had started to sprout new growth. The bushes were turning green before her very eyes, as though the life that had been leeched from them was no longer kept at bay with the dark magic woven here by Gemma. Beside her, Rosie felt her daughter stir.

"Maggie?" she whispered, almost too scared to speak any louder in case her suspicions weren't correct.

But Maggie rolled over, turning her face to meet her mother's. She was wan and tired looking, but she had enough energy to flash her mother a quick smile. "Hey Mom."

Rosie cried out and pulled her close, raining kisses on Maggie's face until her child pulled away from her. "Look—Declan!" Maggie shouted.

Tammy had fallen to her knees in shock not far from where the Declan-statue had stood. They all watched in awe as the stone surrounding him began to crack and crumble, breaking away from the statue piece by piece to reveal a relieved-looking Declan.

"Well *that* was something new and different," he complained lightly, stepping forward and flexing his arms in an experimental stretch. Then he noticed a tear in the waistcoat of his leprechaun costume. "Bloody hell," he added, annoyed. "Now I'll *never* get the deposit back!"

Tammy was gaping up at him, transfixed. "What in the *heck* just happened?" she asked, sounding worried.

Declan quirked a brow. "We're all witches," he said casually with a half-shrug. "Didn't Rosie tell you?"

"*What?!*" Tammy shrieked, making Declan grin. He turned to say something to Rosie, and then noticed that she was still laid out on the new grass that covered the clearing like a promising green blanket. Not so very far away, the ritual dagger was being swallowed by the earth, sinking deeper and deeper beneath the grass until it was no longer there.

"Rosie," he breathed, and ran to her and Maggie followed closely by Tammy.

"I think she drained herself," Maggie said, worried. She pressed a small hand to her mother's brow, but Rosie didn't have the energy to hold her eyes open any longer. She could hear the voices of her friends, but they sounded far away... like she was slipping further and further underwater.

Before that moment, she suddenly realized, she had

been grateful for leaving Randy and Atlanta because of all the things she could get away from. But the real blessing of coming to Mosswood was all the things she was running toward.

Maggie, who was everything to her. Tammy, who was her best friend now whether she liked the idea of being friends with a witch or not. And Declan, who had the potential to be her future. She had chosen each and every one of them, like a museum curator putting together the art that shaped her life. They were her life now. They were who she chose to be.

When Rosie opened her eyes, Maggie, Declan and Tammy surrounded her. They were crouched on the grass, their hands on her body, their eyes closed as they muttered some words she had never heard before. Declan opened his eyes first, meeting Rosie's hazy gaze. A serene smile spread over his handsome face, and Rosie knew that he had gathered everyone together to bring her back from the brink of deathly magical exhaustion. She mustered enough energy to smile back at him.

"Mom!" Maggie threw herself forward, cuddling Rosie tight. She was still weak, but she lifted her arms to hold her daughter close.

"Thought we'd lost you there for a sec," Tammy sighed with relief. "Don't scare us like that, honey!"

"I wasn't worried," Declan lied, rocking back on his heels. "She's too stubborn to leave without havin' the last word."

"Lovely," Rosie mock-glared.

"See?" he grinned, dusting off his hands.

Tammy was looking at Rosie like she was a miracle incarnate—and considering how close Rosie knew she'd come to not being able to make it back to the land of the living, she didn't think it was too far from the truth.

"So," Tammy said matter-of-factly. "You're actually a real-life witch then."

"Yeah," Rosie admitted hesitantly as she sat up, worried about what her friend's reaction would be.

Tammy looked at her for a long minute, and then her face broke into a wicked grin. "Does that mean you can turn Terry into a toad?" She asked suddenly. They both laughed, but then Rosie shrugged.

"Why not? I turned my ex-husband into a turtle."

Tammy stopped laughing, looked at Rosie to see if she was kidding, and then burst out laughing again. "Well, that explains a few things!"

Rosie glanced over to where Declan was showing Maggie how to harness her energy, so that she could pour it into the spell. Then she looked back at Tammy.

"Doesn't it just?"

# CHAPTER SEVENTEEN

I t had been easier for Rosie and Maggie to slowly walk back to the cottage and for Tammy and Declan to take Maude's car back to the town hall than for all of them to try and squash into Maude's ridiculously tiny car. The pair of them had wandered slowly through the woods back towards Fox Cottage with their arms around each other for support and comfort. The plan was to all rendezvous back at the cottage.

"I promised you we'd go trick-or-treating," Rosie told Maggie, pausing by the mailbox and collecting some envelopes out of it. "There's still at least one good solid hour of trick-or-treating left in me. You up for it, Pumpkin?"

They reached the porch. Maggie took the lid off her Jack-o'-lantern and blew out the candle. "Naw," she said. "I think we've had enough excitement for one night, Mom." Rosie smiled sadly, tossing the envelopes on the hall table as they went inside. There was always next year, she supposed.

Maggie was already showered and in bed by the time Declan and Tammy pulled up outside in his truck. Tammy hurried up to the cottage, an gave Rosie a quick hug. "I'm not stoppin'," she advised, already continuing down the hallway. "I definitely need a shower after all that!"

Declan moseyed up to the deck, shuffling his boots in a way that made Rosie think he was just trying to buy himself some time. By the time he'd finally made it to the porch, Rosie was standing on the top step looking down at him. She was tired, and she was sore in more than just one way. Thankfully, he got right to the point.

"I'm no good at makin' speeches," he told her straight, his eyes meeting hers and his expression earnest. "But I *am* good at makin' things right, where I need to. I know I told ya about realizin' you're the one for me, but the truth is, Rosie..." he shook his head for a second, looking into the woods as though to gather his thoughts.

Rosie had just begun to wonder whether he was about to deliver some bad news when he looked back at her again. "I'm done with tryin' to rush into makin' this prophecy happen. I'm done tryin' to please me Da, without worryin' how everyone else feels in the bargain. About how *you* feel."

Rosie paused, took a breath, and then cleared her

throat. "I feel," she said, "like I want to know about how you're going to deal with all the pressure comin' at you from your family. Because I'm not entirely sure that even someone as rebellious as you are can ignore it for all that long."

"I've already dealt with it," he told her. "If you decide that you don't want to join with me to fulfil the prophecy, then I won't do anythin' to change ya mind. I'm not rushing things along anymore, with magic, or booze, or with anything else. If this happens," he said, gesturing between them, "then I want it to happen because it's *right*, not because it's easy."

Rosie looked at him for a long moment, not really sure what she should say next. And then it struck her. She really *did* want Declan in her life... for better or for worse. She just didn't know what that meant for them both right now.

"I don't know anything about joinings, or magical arranged marriages, or prophecies," she shrugged. "But I do know that I want you to be someone in my life that I can trust and count on no matter what. But I can't do that if you don't be straight with me."

He nodded sagely, but she could tell that he was thrilled that she said she wanted him in her life. A smile hovered at the corner of his eyes, threatening to catch the lower half of his face in a crooked grin. "That's fair enough," he said.

"Now that everything's out in the open," Rosie said,

"I'm hoping that we can get down to being us—without the drama on the side."

"I'm hopin' so too," he said, walking up the steps. "I'm sorry that I didn't tell you the truth from the start."

"Me, too," Rosie replied, her face tilting up to his as he stopped on the step below hers. She slipped her arms around his neck and leaned close so that she could whisper against his lips. "But I'm looking forward to starting fresh."

"Seems you have a hankerin' for it," he teased, just before she kissed him lightly. The promise of deepening the kiss presented itself, just as a flash of headlights coming up the drive interrupted them.

"Who in the world can *that* be?" Rosie asked, stepping away from Declan so that she could peer into the darkness. A familiar-looking white SUV pulled up, and Pastor Myles got out. He'd ditched his Jesus costume for a pair of jeans and a light grey pullover, and his hair was styled back in his usual pompadour. As he approached the porch, Rosie could see the light dusting of cuts across his knuckles from where he'd fought with Terry.

"Evenin' folks," he drawled with a smile that was three parts nerves and one part forced courage. "I hope y'all have had a good night, despite the... festivities."

Declan looked at Rosie, and she smiled coyly. "It was... illuminating."

Myles raised his eyebrows but didn't enquire

further. "I'll hope that's a good thing," he teased. "I was actually hopin' to speak to Tammy, if she'll allow it?"

Rosie resisted the urge to holler *Tammy, the Pastor's here for you* at the top of her lungs and dipped her head respectfully instead. "I'll just go tell her you're here," she said. Declan had moved to settle in for the show, leaning a beefy shoulder against the porch support and opening his mouth to ask the Pastor something when he caught the meaningful look Rosie threw his way. "I'd better—erm—go and wash some dishes or somethin'," he said lamely, before following Rosie inside.

Tammy was in the kitchen making mugs of her creamy hot chocolate. She looked up and smiled at them both when they entered.

"Hot chocolates on me!" She finished garnishing them with a cinnamon stick and a shake of nutmeg over the top, and Rosie smiled.

"Declan and I'll share," she said. "You'll need to take two out. Pastor Myles is waiting for you on the porch."

"What!" Tammy breathed, her eyes wide and her cheeks flushing immediately. "Are you sure? I mean, I 'spose you know you're sure, but are you *sure*-sure that he's here to see me, and not just to spread the good word of the Lord? Because sometimes he likes to go out into the community and—"

"Tammy!" Rosie cut her off. "Believe me, hon. He's all puppy-dog eyes and pomade, and he's standing on the porch as we speak." She smirked and nodded her head in the direction of the front porch. "It's not polite to keep him waiting."

Tammy glanced at Rosie, nodded just once, and then almost spilled the hot chocolate in her effort to snatch two up from the counter on her way out of the kitchen. The screen door closed a moment later.

"I wouldn't mind being a fly on the wall for that conversation," Declan mused, lifting the remaining hot chocolate to his lips.

Rosie plucked it from his hand and set it on the counter. "Come on," she whispered.

The pair of them snuck into the living room as quietly as they could without making the floorboards creak to give them away. There was a gap in the middle of the curtains and they peered out together, Declan's head above Rosie's.

Tammy and Myles were sitting next to each other on the top porch step, looking out across the dark lawn. Their legs were angled towards one another, and they were both cradling their mugs of hot chocolate.

"I hope you're not too upset by what all happened this evenin'," Myles said. "We already knew Terry was no-good, from the way he's been actin'. But it was more than just a shock to find out that—" his words faltered, and it looked as though he were trying to get himself together. "—that Priscilla was involved as well." He looked at Tammy, meeting her gaze. "I'm truly sorry."

Tammy swallowed her mouthful of hot chocolate,

and then licked the milk foam from her lips. "You ain't got nothin' to apologize for," she said earnestly. "You're just as blameless as I am in this whole mess. The only ones that need to be apologizin' are him and her, and I don't think either of them's worth listenin' to."

"I don't know if that's true," he said, looking down at his cocoa. "Maybe if I hadn't been so distracted from Prissy..." He looked over at Tammy. "Well, maybe they wouldn't have done it."

"What do you mean 'distracted'?" Tammy asked, though because Rosie was getting to know her better, she thought the woman already knew and just wanted the Pastor to say it.

But she would be disappointed because he didn't say it at all. Instead, his gaze swept Tammy's sweet face, he leaned over, and closed the gap between them with a soft, sweet kiss on her lips. Tammy didn't seem surprised and relaxed into the kiss in a way that told Rosie the two had been smitten with each other for longer than either had the power to admit.

"Awww," she breathed quietly. "Well, it's about time!"

"Halloween," Declan murmured, shaking his head. "No aphrodisiac stronger'n the veil between the dead and the living being at its thinnest." He hooked his thumb under Rosie's chin, and tilted her lips towards his so that he could claim them in a kiss.

They exited the living room hand in hand, still being careful not to disturb the peace on the porch. As they passed the hall table, Rosie snatched the pile of mail up. Might as well get the bad news over and done with, while sipping on the liquid heaven that was Tammy's hot chocolate.

Declan got two spoons out of the cutlery draw for eating the foam with, as Rosie looked at the first envelope on the pile. It was official-looking. She tore it open, read the first few lines, and then sighed as her forgotten life crept back into the one she'd built for herself.

"What?" Declan asked, immediately concerned. She let the letter flutter to the counter, where Declan could see the bold typed block letters across the top of the letter.

EVICTION NOTICE

"But you always pay your rent on time," Declan argued, preparing to get fired up. "They can't just evict you for no good reason!"

Rosie met his gaze, the hot chocolate forgotten on the counter.

"It's not for me," she announced. "We're not being evicted from Fox Cottage." She looked down at the letter again. "It's for Randy's old apartment in Atlanta."

# Thanks for reading

Thank you so much for joining me for the second instalment of my *Midlife in Mosswood* series - I hope you enjoyed it!

Halloween has always been my favourite holiday (despite living in Australia, where it's hardly celebrated), and I have loved jumping into my first true American Halloween, even if it's only by way of my imagination.

I've included a bonus short story in the following pages just for a giggle. Witch and Moan takes place right after Jealousy's A Witch, and follows the antics of Tammy's husband, Terry, after the events of the Mosswood Harvest Ball.

We Witch You A Merry Christmas will be book three in the series. We'll find out what Rosie has waiting for her in Atlanta, what the fallout from book two looks like for Tammy and Myles, and end the book with an 'awww!' moment that's been a long time coming. Read on for an exclusive sneak peek at the first chapter.

Stay cool, and be kind to yourself.

Louisa xo

## Bless your heart

I am nothing without my posse.

Thank you once again to my fabulous editor, Kimberly Jaye. Without her, I would be a plotless mess on the floor.

Thank you to my wonderful partner, Lindsay, who quite literally dropped everything to proof-read this book in less than 24 hours. Not only is he dedicated, he's really damn good at pointing out typos.

Thank you to my ARC readers, who are amazingly supportive and helpful - I'm so grateful that you were happy to read another Rosie book!

Thanks to my beautiful mum, who might not love every scene I write, but who's wonderfully supportive none-the-less. (I'll tell you when to skip the sexy parts, Mum, I promise.)

And thank you once again to my daughter, whose joyful presence makes writing about a mother-daughter bond that more delightful.

## Love it? Review it!

A reader writing a review for a book is such a gift to an author. Not only does it let us know that someone out there actually read the thing, but it's so heart-warming to think that they enjoyed it enough to offer their thoughts on it afterwards.

If you've enjoyed this book, I would be so grateful if you'd consider leaving me a review! You can do this by searching for the book title and my name on Amazon.com or on GoodReads and then following the prompts.

If you're a book-blogger, bookstagrammer, or journalist and you would like to interview me, please get in touch with me at www.louisawest.com - I would love to chat with you!

Free Midlife in Mosswood story

# WITCH
## AND MOAN

## A MIDLIFE IN MOSSWOOD STORY

Available now on Amazon and in Kindle Unlimited

https://books2read.com/wwyamc

## Witch And Moan

Thank *fuck* he'd brought his own booze to the party. The whole damn thing had been a bust from start to finish, and the only thing that had saved it was his special-brewed moonshine burning the shit out of his throat as he swallowed mouthful after mouthful. He reckoned it was the only way to cauterize the infectious, sickly-sweet words he'd been forced to spew up throughout the evening, first to his wife, then to his girlfriend. By the time he'd been knocked on his ass by Jesus, he'd been glad to get the hell outta Dodge.

Well. A preacher masquerading in a Jesus costume. If that wasn't sacrilegious as all get-out then he didn't know what was!

He had stumbled down the steps of the Mosswood town hall, his eye and nose smarting and his head swimming with mean thoughts that his even meaner hands had every intention of carrying out. He'd swiped three bottles of cheap light beer from the party as he'd exited, and now cradled them in one arm as he wandered up Lee Street towards their precious Church. It sat high on its perch above the town, judging all and sundry while the untouchable Baptist folk of Mosswood got away with all manner of sins.

He oughta know. He used to be one of them.

But the tide had turned, it seemed. He wasn't the sort to lick his wounds quietly—never had been. He muttered darkly to himself about witches and black magic and people being under the influence of spells as he staggered up the hill towards the Church. The moon hung low in the cloudy sky above and leaves scattered across the path in front of him, whipped into a flurry by that persistent kind of breeze that seemed reserved for spooky nights. It brought with it the ghostly sound of children's laughter, which was swallowed only moments later by the old oak trees on either side of the street bending and creaking.

He wasn't sure if it was the moonshine or the shiner on his face, but as he neared the Churchyard the air seemed to get thinner. By the time he'd reached the intricate, wrought-iron gates set into the brick wall that surrounded the Mosswood Cemetery, he was tired enough to stop walking and ready enough to cause some trouble. After rattling the lock on the gates, he could only see one way around it. He stuffed a bottle of beer in each of the back pockets of his Levi's and gripped the neck of the other in his teeth before lodging his boot between two of the bars in the gate.

Varsity football never seemed so far in his past as it did in that moment. With a grunt that denoted more effort than he'd made for anything since his last sprint on the field, he hoisted himself up into a standing position on the gates. A slosh of beer dribbled down the back of one of his legs and he scowled. He cussed under his breath as he climbed to the top, the gate swinging wildly beneath his considerable weight. More beer was sloshed. More cuss words were growled into the midnight air.

By the time he reached the top of the gate he wasn't so sure this had been a great idea after all, but he'd be damned if he would give up now. He swung one thick leg over the top, carefully avoiding the pointed spikes on the bars that had been designed to keep out less-skilled intruders than him. He smirked, grabbing hold of the beer bottle he had in his mouth and tilting it back. He drained it with four large gulps, threw the bottle carelessly onto the grass below as he swallowed the last of it, and then let out a huge burp that echoed through the graveyard.

"Take *that*, you fuckin' hypocrites!" he slurred, reaching down to adjust his manhood away from a spike that was encroaching on his personal space. He barked a deep, menacing laugh, holding on to the top of the gate and swinging his other leg over the side. And that was where he met his maker—figuratively speaking.

A spike snagged the fabric of his jeans, slipping through the well-worn weave with ease. It disrupted the momentum of his leg swing, causing him to overbalance. He gripped the gate desperately, over-correcting. The spike got sick of the taste of denim, biting into the doughy flesh of his thigh instead. He yipped with pain, fumbled, and let go of the gate. There was a long, solid *riiiiiiip* as his only good pair of jeans tore straight down the leg, but that was the least of his worries. The rest of him was soaked with cheap beer as he fell, and when he landed on the grass below, the two bottles in his back pockets broke his fall. Somewhat.

"Aaaargh!" he cried out, pain coursing through his body from a variety of places. He didn't know whether to be more concerned about the spasms in his back or the hot stinging of the broken glass in his ass cheeks, but in the end he settled for a combination of the two. He lay still for a moment before slowly rolling onto his belly, at which point he was able to use the remainder of his moonshine-addled brain to stand up gingerly. He pressed a hand to his butt, seeing his blood shining darkly in the moonlight when he lifted it to his face.

Enraged, he leant down to retrieve the other beer bottle he'd thrown on the grass and pegged it straight at the nearest tombstone in a fit of rage.

"That fuckin' bitch!" he yelled. "That fuckin' weird-ass, no-good, meddlin' *witch* bitch!"

The already thin air shimmered around him, and for a moment he wondered whether he was starting to feel woozy from the booze, a possible concussion, blood loss from his ass—or a combination of all three. A fourth option presented itself as he watched a small white light rise up from the ground in front of the tombstone he had just thrown the bottle at; wispy tendrils of some kind of glowing ectoplasmic spoke unfurled until an elderly woman wearing a frilled cap and an apron was glaring at him.

Nope. Options one-through-three were a bust. He'd just straight up lost his damn mind.

She looked incredibly real aside from the fact that she was completely see-through and that she faded away to nothing right where her feet ought to be. His eyes grew as wide as saucers, and he gaped at her in surprise. It would be highly unlikely for the Church to hire projectors of ghosts for the Cemetery on Halloween, but it was the only logical explanation and he was holding on to it with both of his calloused hands. He'd just managed to convince himself that he must have tripped the projection sensor by stumbling too near it when the woman spoke to him.

"I'll be askin' you to kindly take that language elsewhere, young man!" she huffed, the edges of her voice colored with the hints of a soft Irish accent. "And clean up that glass! Immediately!"

He gaped at her, his mouth slightly open. His breath, blood pressure, and heart rate were all rising faster than he'd hit the deck after falling from the gate.

She levelled her gaze at him and shook her head.

"How far do you have to fall before you pick your sorry behind up again, Terry Holt?" she asked, glancing over at the gate and then back to him. "Surely you hit rock-bottom just about now."

"Wh-who *are* you?" Terry stammered, watching the woman nervously. "Ma'am," he added with all due haste.

The woman gestured to the tombstone that Terry had flung his empty beer bottle at. Aside from a scrape where the glass had grazed the granite, the only other mark on it was the inscription:

Geraldine May Holt
1859—1918
Beloved wife, mother, and grandmother
Resting peacefully until God reunites us in the hereafter

"Great-great-great Grandmother Holt?!" he asked incredulously, looking from the inscription to her and back again.

"That's right," she said, clasping her hands primly in front of her apron. "I didn't survive a civil war, nigh-on starvation, and the Spanish Lady only to be roused from my sleep by one of my own ancestors actin' a fool and desecratin' a grave!" She tutted. "If you're not already ashamed of yourself, you oughta be!"

All his pain was temporarily forgotten in the midst of this weird and terrifying exchange. Sure enough, the woman had the famous Holt brow ('as wide as it was stubborn,' his mother used to say). He offered her a gesture that was half of a shrug and half of an apology, his hands lifted in front of him.

"I'm sorry!" he told her, feeling his knees shake uncertainly. "I didn't mean to! I—"

"—always have yourself an excuse, yes I know," she interrupted him wryly. She stretched an arm out, tenderly placing a hand atop the grave of her husband beside her. "But I'm not just talkin' about the destruction. Or the swearing. Or the *drinking*," she added, waving her other hand under her wrinkled nose to dispel the stench of second-hand moonshine and spilled beer. "I'm talkin' about the unwholesome life you been livin'. Bein' unfaithful to your beautiful wife."

She shook her head sadly. "We watched you get married, you know. From right here, we watched the pair of you come out of that Church, and I said to the good Lord then that you didn't deserve her." And then a gleam sparked in her ghostly eye, and a slow smile spread across her face. "Oh, but you'll get yours, and no mistake. There's a special place in Hell reserved for adulterers, my boy."

"I've tried to repent!" he bleated, sounding like a sheep who had followed selfishness its whole life instead of its shepherd only to be surprised to find itself heading for slaughter. "I've begged her to take me back, but she won't! It's that *damn* Rosemary Bell! She—"

"Has nothing to do with your wandering eye," Grandma Holt cut him off, "—or your fickle affection.

This is a mess entirely of your own makin', and so must be the remedy. True redemption comes with a change for the better, young man. And unless you offer yourself up in repentance, you're a lost cause I'm afraid."

Terry fell to his knees, clasping his hands together and ignoring the searing pain across his ass. "But I don't want to go to Hell! Please, help me!" he begged. "Please! I'll do anything!"

His great-great-great grandmother looked down her nose at him, seeming to consider his plea. At long last she sighed and crossed her arms over her chest. "Very well," she said. "I'll help you. But only because I hate the thought of having to spend eternity with *you* coasting around this graveyard every Halloween because you don't like it down where you're headed," she scolded. "We all like to get together once a year and catch up on the latest happenings, and we don't want anyone bringin' down the mood!"

Terry blinked, looking around the graveyard. "But there's no one else here."

"Not right now there isn't," she sighed. "Scared off by your pathetic display of fragile masculinity, I suspect. Now do you want my help, or are you more inclined to keep fillin' the air with the sound of your own voice?"

"Sorry," he apologised quickly. "Please! I don't wanna go to Hell!"

She raised a spectral eyebrow in his direction, but otherwise maintained her excellent composure. "Very well. Stop thinkin' of yourself before you think of others," she began, ticking off a finger, "stop actin' like the world owes you a living, because it most certainly doesn't," she ticked off another finger. "And last but definitely not least—stop drinking!" Third finger ticked off and hands now clasped, she smirked at her descendent. "That ought to about do it!"

Terry blinked. "Is that it?" he asked ungratefully.

She shrugged a shoulder, and then rolled her eyes. "Very well—a bonus, then. You had better see the town surgeon for some stitches in your derriere."

"Some fat lot of good that all is gonna get me!" Terry blustered, his fear dimming only to be replaced with the anger that was never far beneath his surface. He gestured towards the entrance of the Cemetery. "Can't you at least magic open the damned gate?"

"No," she shook her head. "I'm afraid that's not possible."

"Why not?" he asked her. "Aren't you an all-knowing spirit from beyond? If you can appear here on Halloween," Terry sassed, "why can't you just open a lock on a gate?"

"Oh I didn't say I *couldn't*," Grandmother Holt told him, and then smirked wickedly. "But it was far too much fun watching you climb over it in the first place to deprive myself of the joy of seeing you navigate it a second time. It's no more and certainly not less than you deserve."

He was so shocked by this revelation that he didn't

really know what to say. Eventually he muttered a gruff "Thanks for nothing, then!" as he carried himself over to the gate. It had already been a night to forget in a hurry, and the sooner he managed to stop his butt from bleeding, the better. Without ceremony and fuelled by embarrassment and that stubbornness his whole family was known for, Terry hoisted himself up onto the gate once more. The contraction of muscles around shards of glass made him howl with pain, and he took a few quick breaths before turning back to say something absolutely rotten to his long-dead ancestor.

But the graveyard was empty.

With his dignity as shredded as his jeans and his hide, Terry navigated the gate and landed on the other side after a gate-spike had stabbed a hole in the sleeve of his shirt for good measure. As he limped off down the hill back into downtown Mosswood a gentle whooshing sound filled the Cemetery. Slivers of ectoplasmic smoke began to curl up from each of the graves, growing and taking shape until all of Mosswood's former residents from across the ages were present and accounted for.

"Do you think he'll take his lumps and learn from 'em," Nathaniel, Terry's great-great-great Grandfather asked, holding the crook of his arm out for his wife.

"No," she replied, slipping her arm into her husband's. She turned to a plump woman who was fussing with the collar of a young boy, smoothing it down as though they needed to look their best. "I'm sorry, Violet," Geraldine said to her. "It must be terribly upsetting."

Violet smiled a tight little smile, not looking up from her attention to the boy's collar. "Oh, don't you worry about my Tammy," she said. "That's a girl who can look out for herself."

Your next Mosswood adventure awaits!

# WE WITCH
## YOU A MERRY CHRISTMAS

MIDLIFE IN MOSSWOOD BOOK 3

Available now on Amazon and in Kindle Unlimited

https://books2read.com/wwyamc

## We Witch You A Merry Christmas

**All she wants for Christmas is some peace and quiet. But Santa—and the local sheriff's office—might just have her on the naughty list.**

Rosemary Bell's got a brand new bag. She has a great circle of friends, a sexy Irish boyfriend, and a daughter following in her witchy footsteps. But when she becomes the prime suspect in her grinch husband's disappearance, the halls she'll be decking might be behind bars.

Things get even bleaker when she's called home to clean up her husband's mess. When Rosie finds clues about a family she never knew she had, she realizes she doesn't know as much about her past as she thought. And her present isn't much better, when the local sheriff joins the investigation into her crimes.

With the local Sheriff breathing down her neck, it'll take a Christmas miracle to keep her new family together for the holidays. This year Rosie might find herself witching for a Merry Christmas.

***Charmed* meets *The Santa Clause* in this short novel about the families we're born into, the families we choose, and the magic of Christmas.**

**AVAILABLE DECEMBER 15**
**PREORDER:** https://books2read.com/wwyamc

## We Witch You A Merry Christmas - Chapter One

"Wait, so she's just lurking upstairs in the master bedroom like the wife from Jane Eyre?"

Rosie stared at Tammy in disbelief. They huddled together over the kitchen island in the middle of the Bishop family home. Rosie artfully arranged parsley around the turkey while Tammy scooped stuffing to make it look like it had cooked inside it and not in the baking dish next to it. Pumpkins and gourds in all shapes, colors, and sizes piled around them, stacked with bright red apples and fake autumn foliage. Rosie suspected the owner of the kitchen had chosen the decor more to get in Tammy's way than to look festive for Thanksgiving.

Maybe Priscilla Bishop wasn't just haunting the attic.

Tammy whispered as she worked.

"Myles has moved into one of the guest rooms for now. She keeps trying to stall signing the divorce papers." She sighed as she stood upright and looked plaintively at Rosie. "Bless her heart."

"Well," Rosie declared, stuffing parsley under a drumstick as though it had insulted her somehow. "I don't feel sorry for her one bit. She made her bed."

Tammy sighed again and looked around the kitchen wistfully. "Reckon she'll wanna keep the house," she said before leaning forward to pick up the turkey. Despite the bird being the size of a small car, she picked it up with ease and headed for the swinging door that led to the formal dining room. "I sure wouldn't mind having this kitchen."

With the swish of the door, the two women and the world around them shifted. The kitchen was the realm of gossip and heart to hearts. The dining room was the realm of holiday cheer and food comas.

The home's central staircase overlooked the formal dining room and was so grand-looking it might as well have led to the pearly gates. The polished dining table housed a dozen side dishes atop a simple red table runner. The only decoration on the table was the two poinsettias Rosie had brought as a hostess gift for Myles and Tammy, breathed back to life from the clearance section at Walmart. Myles, Declan, Ben, and Maggie cheered as Tammy added the piece de resistance to the table's center.

"Oh, now stop," Tammy beamed. "You'll make me blush."

"This is nothing short of heavenly," Myles said as Tammy sat beside him, and then she really did blush.

"Look, Mom," Maggie announced excitedly. "Mac and cheese! My favorite!"

"I know," Rosie grinned at her daughter. "It's a Thanksgiving miracle!" Tammy's feminine giggle sounded from her right.

"Thanks for inviting us," Ben added, though his gaze never left the food. He might as well have been thanking the turkey. It didn't matter; the host's eyes were all for Tammy.

"It wouldn't be the same without y'all," Myles said with an easy smile. When he finally looked away from Tammy, he surveyed the table with real kindness. "I'm a fortunate man to have so many good people to share my blessings with."

At those words, Declan looked to Rosie. Their gazes met, and he reached for her hand under the table. For a moment, there was no world outside of the two of them. He didn't say it—he wasn't as good with words as Myles—but the sentiment shone in his sea-colored eyes. I'm a fortunate man, too.

Myles had received a nod of approval from Tammy, reaching for her hand on his right and Rosie's hand to his left as he prepared to say grace. He took a breath as Declan, Ben, and Maggie joined in and was just about to start speaking when the doorbell rang.

It was the most pretentious doorbell chime that Rosie had ever heard in her life. The first bar of Amazing Grace rang out through the whole house, and everyone's heads swiveled in that direction. Myles hesitated, torn between saying Grace and getting up to answer the door. The chime was beginning to fade into memory when whoever pressed the doorbell again.

The sound of shuffling of feet on the staircase overhead heralded in the Ghost of Thanksgiving Hostesses Past. Six pairs of eyes turned upward to watch Prissy swan down the sweeping stairs and into the foyer. She held her pointed nose in the air despite her baby-blue silk robe and white fluffy slippers.

Rosie's eyes bulged as she swiveled her gaze to Tammy. Myles hung his head and kept his hands held to either side of him as they waited for the noise to pass.

"Evening, Mrs. Bishop! Veggie Supreme, no tomato, no onion, extra olives, extra Parmesan?"

Maggie sat up straighter. "Are we having pizza, too?"

"No!" the adults all whispered back in sync.

"Thank you, Al," Prissy sounded resigned. The tell-tale sound of a pizza box exchanging hands drifted into the dining room. "It's not exactly turkey dinner... but we make do."

Al sounded awkward. "Er, yes, Mrs. Bishop. Happy Thanksgiving."

"You, too, Al."

Rosie rolled her eyes at the pathetic note Prissy

added to her voice, then shoved the look away when the woman reappeared clutching the pizza box. Her eyes matched the color of her robe so perfectly it was unnerving, as she glared at the company assembled round the table. She marched forward and stationed herself between Tammy and Myles. With an unceremonious plop that shook the plates, she added her pizza to the smorgasbord.

"May I join the prayer?" she asked.

Rosie realized she was holding her breath. She forced herself to exhale before flicking her eyes in the direction of Myles and Tammy.

Myles glanced at Tammy. Tammy glanced at Myles. And at last, the pastor lowered his chin and let go of Tammy's hand. "Of course," he said. Rosie was impressed that it only sounded a little bit like he was gritting his teeth. Prissy took each of their hands in turn, and Myles lowered his head again.

"Heavenly Father, thank you for this day. Thank you for this food we are about to eat. Thank you for our good health, for our talents, and for the opportunity to dedicate those things to the service of others. Thank you for the embrace of your love and the love of our family and friends." He paused, and Rosie thought for a moment he might be done, but then he continued.

"—and Lord, please bless those who are not fortunate enough to have family and friends to celebrate with today. Bless-this-food and nourish-it-to-our-bodies, in-Jesus'-name-we-pray, amen."

"Amen," the rest of them chorused... except for Prissy.

She glared at him, looking like she had more to say before she seemed to think better of it. Instead, she spat out a very un-Christian-like 'amen' and turned on her heel, leaving the room with her robe flaring behind her.

Myles tracked Prissy's movement until she was out of sight. Tammy laid a soft hand on top of his, and Myles blinked out of his glare. He looked around the table and offered them all a more forced version of his boyish smile.

"Don't let it get any colder, y'all. Dig in!"

Declan and Maggie didn't need to be told twice and started helping themselves to the plates on the table. Myles stood to carve the turkey.

Prissy would have been disappointed to learn how quickly she was forgotten. Tammy's infectious cheer and Maggie's enthusiasm were catching. As the eating slowed, Rosie caught Tammy's eyes across the table.

"I'm leaving this table stuffed fuller than that bird," she grinned, nodding at the turkey.

"Wouldn't have it any other way," Tammy cooed. "It's not a fit start to the holiday season otherwise!"

Myles huffed a quiet laugh. "I can't believe it's nearly the end of the year," he mused. "Where did the time go?"

"Where all time goes," Maggie said, picking at the food left on her plate. She let her voice drop in tone to more closely match her mother's and lifted her brows. "Straight out the window!'"

Ben chuckled along with the others, but looked full enough to pop.

"Well," Tammy said, "I think it's been a lovely year, even if it was difficult at times." She shot a glance at Myles, but then moved forward, glass in hand. "I'm grateful for the blessing of starting over."

"Hear, hear," Rosie agreed, and the two shared a smile.

"I'm grateful the Go-Go is doing well enough to keep more help on," Ben said, nodding his head at Rosie. She grinned.

"Oh, I'm grateful for that, too." A good-natured chuckle went up around the table from the adults.

"I'm grateful," Myles said, in a thoughtful way, "for expunging the bad, so I can start building a little good." He wiped the tips of his fingers on a napkin. "It's been a rough year, and it'd sure be nice for things to settle down enough to just be content without puttin' out spot fires."

Tammy was looking at Myles, her eyes like beacons of the feelings she had for him. She chewed her food, debating whether to share.

"I'm also grateful... for the opportunity to learn about who I am without bein' 'Mrs. Tammy Holt'," she said, hesitantly at first but then seeming to gain more courage. "I have a ways to go, of course. But I'm confident that I can start by finalizing my divorce papers and figurin' out what to do with Terry's shop."

Tammy's gaze slowly drifted back to Myles, who looked thrilled that she was willing to forge her way forward. More than that, Rosie thought. He looks like he's ready to go along for that ride with her.

"I'm grateful for turkey," Declan interrupted the moment, and Rosie rolled her eyes. Declan held up his knife and fork, which still sported a hefty slice of white meat. "Laugh all ya want. We don't get much turkey back home. I intend to live it up while I can!"

Rosie was still shaking her head when Tammy turned the attention onto her. "What about you, Rosie?"

Yes, Rosie. What about you?

"Oh, uh…" Rosie glanced around the table, feeling her silence draw out. She looked at Ben, who had given her a job and financial independence, then to Tammy and to the man that made her happy. Finally, Rosie's gaze landed on Maggie and the hulking Irishman sitting next to her.

"I'm grateful for all of you," she said at last. She felt the threatening sting behind her eyes that told her she'd better lighten the mood, and added, "Although, I'd also be grateful for a washing machine in the house."

The awkwardness lifted, and Tammy raised her glass in a toast. "Amen to that!"

Maggie puffed out her chest, proud to share. "Well, I'm thankful for the new iPad we get to share in class.

By next summer, I'll be so smart I won't ever have to go back to school," she announced.

"Good luck with that one, wee'an," Declan grinned.

"It'd be nice if you started with turning in your homework on time," Rosie agreed.

"It's not my fault that Da—" Maggie paused, correcting herself, "—that my turtle keeps ripping it up!" She frowned in protest.

"That's true," Rosie said. "But it is your fault that you leave it where the turtle can get to it in the first place."

The conversation flowed, interspersed with gentle laughter. It moved to the subject of Christmas, as Thanksgiving dinner so often does.

"Do you think we could maybe have a real tree this year?" Maggie asked around a mouthful of her third helping of mac and cheese.

Rosie felt her stomach plummet. She was already going to be pushing it to afford a small fake tree, and she had been keeping an eye out online and in the local newspaper in case anyone was selling a second-hand one.

"We'll have to see what's available, Pumpkin," she said. She stacked the plates of those who were finished eating.

"They have real trees at the Pineview Christmas Market," Tammy said helpfully, making Rosie want to strangle her.

Maggie's face lit up. "Could we go, Mom? Please?"

Rosie glanced sideways at Tammy, who realized her faux-pas too late and went back to tidying the table. "We'll see," Rosie said, in a tone that Maggie would recognize as meaning 'if we have the money.'

"Well," Maggie said, matter-of-factly. "I don't really mind about the tree so much. I only have one Christmas wish."

"Don't tell us," Tammy warned, a spatula flashing through the air, "or it won't come true!"

"It's got more chance of comin' true if I tell people about it than if I don't," Maggie said.

Rosie hid a smile at her child's sound logic. "What's the wish?"

Maggie beamed. "My wish is for snow for Christmas!" she announced.

*Well, shit*, Rosie thought.

THE CHRISTMAS RUSH BEGAN IN EARNEST THE FRIDAY after turkey day. Black Friday sales meant an influx of customers at the Go-Go Mart and more shifts for Rosie. While she wasn't sorry about earning the extra cash, she did feel as though she was missing out on time with Maggie. She supposed she couldn't have it both ways. Work would settle down after the New Year, and she was hoping to save enough to get Maggie a bike for Christmas in the meantime. It wouldn't be snow, but it would be something useful, at any rate.

Saturday morning, Rosie recognized the sound of Declan's truck rumbling up the drive to Fox Cottage. She glanced up from the local news on her phone to focus on the coffee pot across the kitchen. The familiar buzz of magical energy hummed around her, and seconds later, the cold coffee was steaming.

"Coffee's hot," she announced as Declan closed the front door behind him. She returned her attention to the article about the Pineview Christmas market.

"Ah, you're an angel," he sighed as he fixed himself a cup. "Had to make an emergency resupply this morning, and I'm wiped."

"There's stuff to make a sandwich in the fridge, too —and some apples."

He gulped a mouthful of coffee and then recoiled when it was a little too hot for comfort. He smiled anyway. "What would I do without you?" he asked as he leaned his hip against the counter.

Rosie raised an amused eyebrow at him. "Die from starvation and caffeine withdrawal?"

He smirked.

She wrapped her hands around her warm mug. "Thanks for offering to drive us out to the Plantation today."

"Happy to help out my girls." He stood a little straighter and inspected his coffee. "In fact, I've been thinking…"

"—always a worry," Rosie interrupted.

"—I was thinking," he started again, "It's startin' to

get colder in the mornings, and Tammy says it'll be getting wet soon, too. I thought it'd be good if I started drivin' Miss Maggie to school in the mornings—and you, when you work the morning shift. That way, ya won't have to walk there and back twice over in the cold. I might not always be able to pick you up in the afternoons, dependin' on my delivery route. But I can cover the mornings, at least. Startin' Monday."

Gratitude flooded Rosie's heart at the sweetness of the gesture. She couldn't help comparing him to Randy and how he wouldn't have even been around in the mornings when Maggie was getting ready for school. His gang had always seemed more important than parenting duties—or husbanding duties for that matter. What a difference a man made.

When she didn't answer him right away, Declan filled the silence hastily. "Maybe Tammy could drive you home in the afternoons? I'm sure she wouldn't mind. And some afternoons, I definitely could do the pickups. Just not on the days I need to get to and from Huntsville—"

Rosie stepped up to Declan, relishing the look of pleasant surprise on his face as she slipped her arms around his waist. She stood on tiptoe to press a soft, slow kiss to his lips. His arms folded around her, and he leaned into the kiss so that when she pulled away, his eyes were still closed and his lips still half-puckered. It was vulnerable and adorable, and by the time he opened his eyes to look down into her face, Rosie was smiling up at him.

"Thank you," she murmured. "That's so sweet and considerate of you, and Maggie and I both appreciate it a lot."

"Well," he said, squaring his shoulders and puffing out his chest in a way that told Rosie he wasn't used to being genuinely thanked for anything. "Wouldn't be much of a Prince Charmin' if I can't offer my noble steed to—"

"—if you even think about saying 'save a damsel in distress', I'll make what that turtle did to you look weak." Rosie reached to collect her coffee mug and put it in the sink.

Declan grunted at the unpleasant memory. He turned to grab things from the fridge to make himself a sandwich. Rosie went to her purse to check that she'd have everything she'd need for an afternoon at Pineview Plantation's annual Christmas market.

Wallet? Check. Gloves? Check. Eviction notice for the apartment she used to share with her ex-husband? Sigh.

"What do you think I should do about this?" she asked, holding it out to Declan. He took it, clamping his freshly made sandwich between his teeth to unfold the paper before taking a bite as he started to read.

"Figured you'd decided to ignore it," he told her with a half-shrug that didn't hide the spark of curiosity in his eyes.

"Guess I sort of did," she agreed, leaning against the counter. "But there's something about it that's gnawing at me."

He handed the paper back to her. "Was your name on the lease?"

She shook her head. "Randy would never let me have that much of a say in anything we did," she added.

"Then you can't owe anything on the apartment," he said. "So that's one upside to him being a controlling wanker. What else could be worryin' ya?"

Rosie searched her brain for the real reason she had hung onto the eviction notice.

"I guess I just feel sad to leave absolutely everything we had there," she said at last. "There were a lot of Maggie's toys that we just didn't have time to pack and bring with us, and..."

She drifted off, getting more uncomfortable talking the closer they got to the root of her feelings.

"And," he prompted gently, his sandwich-free hand seeking one of hers.

"And," she continued, finally releasing the sigh that she hadn't wanted to let out. "All of our Christmas decorations are in a box in that apartment. None of them are expensive, but there are a few little ones that Maggie made when she was younger that I'd like to have kept." She shrugged, feeling lost. "It seems pointless to have a huge Christmas tree when I don't even have any ornaments to put on it, let alone the ones that mean something to me."

Declan was frowning, his lips pressed together in concentration as he tried to find a solution to the growing mound of problems. "Would you rather not go tree shopping today?" he asked her. "We could do something else fun with Maggie instead?"

Rosie shook her head. "No way. Maggie's counting on it, and I would hate to disappoint her—but I feel like I'll do that anyway!" Frustration nibbled persistently at her last nerve, and she tried to shrug it off unsuccessfully.

"What do you mean you'll disappoint her anyway?" Declan asked.

She opened her mouth to reply, but nothing came out. He stepped closer.

"Hey," he comforted her, putting down the rest of his sandwich so that he could sweep her up in a hug. He held her close, his hands stroking her back soothingly. "You could never disappoint Maggie! Anyone with eyes in their head can see the wee'an adores you."

Rosie looked up at him, then squared her shoulders, creating some space.

"Okay," she declared in a steady voice. "I'm going to tell you something, and you aren't allowed to make pitying noises, or say how much it sucks, or feel sorry for me in any way. I'm only telling you so you understand where I'm coming from."

Declan had heard this speech so many times by now

that he no longer questioned it. He schooled his face and nodded his head. "Shoot."

Rosie took a breath and began. "Randy had this thing about Christmas. Every year, I tried to make the best of it with whatever little money I had. But then he would go out and blow all the cash he wouldn't let me have access to, and he'd waltz in on Christmas morning with these amazing gifts for Maggie. I stressed all season, and he looked like the hero."

She grounded herself by placing two hands on either of Declan's pecs, because if she had to ground herself, she might as well be entertained while she did it.

"Christmas was miserable every year," she continued. "This is our first Christmas without him, and I want to make it a special one. And maybe…. I don't know, actually enjoy Christmas myself."

She looked up at him. Declan nodded until he was sure she was finished and then pulled her back into his embrace.

"Well, then," he said finally, leaning down to kiss her tenderly on the forehead. "Why don't we start by going and gettin' this kid her Christmas tree today, and then going to Atlanta to get your stuff?"

"Really?" Rosie leaned back so that she could look up at him, her fears momentarily silenced.

He smiled, that dimple in his cheek coming out in full force. "Absolutely. We can go next week on your day off, while Maggie's at school. And then you can surprise her when she gets home."

Calm flooded her frayed nerves. "That would be wonderful," she said. "Thank you."

He was such a welcome distraction from her darker thoughts, and she indulged in glimpsing at his broad shoulders. He noticed her staring. The heat in his look reflected hers, and Rosie felt a smirk tug at her lips.

Maybe there was something she wanted more than her very own washing machine after all.

"Maggie!" she called, though her eyes were still pinned to his. "Declan's here to drive us to the tree farm!"

"Coming, Mom!"

Rosie circled her arms around Declan's waist and leaned against him.

"Let's go get some wood."

Maggie appeared as Declan was choking back his reaction. There was a knock at the door, and Rosie loosed her hold on her Irish beefcake to answer it. Behind her, she heard Maggie voice 'concern' for him.

"You're supposed to swallow it, not inhale it."

Rosie snorted as she opened the front door.

Carol-Ann Wallace stood on the porch, her thin shoulders hunched together to ward off the cold. Light rain dusted the lawn, and Rosie almost groaned to think they would be out in the cold and the wet at Pineview.

"Oh! Hi Carol-Ann." Rosie blinked, opening the screen door, too. "Is something wrong?"

Though she was an older lady, Carol-Ann still seemed sharp as a tack. Her hawk-like eyes took in the new paint on the cottage and the porch repairs Declan had done in the fall, but they lingered on Rosie's flourishing garden. The winter greenery was the picture of health, and Rosie was especially proud of the holly growing on either side of the porch steps.

"Yes and no," Carol-Ann said with reluctant approval. She held a wilted houseplant aloft before her and then shrugged. "Elladine down at The Moon Café said you fixed her fiddle-leaf fig right as rain, and if I kill my mother's prize orchid while she's in Florida, she will never forgive me."

"Oh," Rosie exclaimed, reaching to take the plant from Carol-Ann. She held it aloft to take a look at the leaves and then hummed with understanding. She tucked the pot onto one hip the way she had used to carry Maggie when she was small.

"I'll see what I can do," she smiled.

"Five percent off your rent if you can manage it," Carol-Ann nodded, "And five percent off my life if you can't."

She started down the steps while Rosie started to tally how much five percent of her rent was. But then she noticed something through the rain. She squinted out into the yard.

A large jeep with Mosswood Sheriff Department badging on it pulled away from her driveway, back toward town.

# MIDLIFE IN
# MOSSWOOD

## PARANORMAL WOMEN'S FICTION SERIES

# LOUISA WEST

## Also by Louisa West

### THE MIDLIFE IN MOSSWOOD SERIES

New Witch on the Block

https://books2read.com/nwotb

Jealousy's A Witch

https://books2read.com/jaw

We Witch You A Merry Christmas

https://books2read.com/wwyamc

Get Witch Quick

https://books2read/gwq

Son of a Witch

https://books2read/sofaw

# About the author

Louisa likes Pina Coladas and gettin' caught in the rain. Determined to empty her brain of stories, she loves writing Paranormal Women's Fiction and other stories about kick-ass women doing whatever the hell they want to do.

She lives in Mandurah, Western Australia, and drinks more coffee than is good for her. When she's not writing or researching projects, Louisa enjoys spending time with her family, and Harriet The Great (Dane). Hobbies include playing video games, watching copious amounts of tv, and various craft-related initiatives.

She strongly believes that the truth is still out there.

Are you interested in:

- New release information and pre-order links
- Competitions, giveaways, and other freebies
- Sneak peeks at cover reveals and excerpts
- VIP access to online launch parties and
- Exclusive member rewards

Then join Louisa's online reader group at
www.facebook.com/groups/magicalmayhem!

facebook.com/louisawestauthor

instagram.com/louisa_west

amazon.com/author/louisawest

goodreads.com/louisawest

pinterest.com/louisawestauthor

CPSIA information can be obtained
at www.ICGtesting.com
Printed in the USA
LVHW112348081022
730276LV00001B/100